LORI WICK

As Time Goes By

HARVEST HOUSE PUBLISHERS
Eugene, Oregon 97402

Scripture verses are taken from the King James Version of the Bible.

Except for certain well-established place names, all names of persons and places mentioned in this novel are fictional.

Cover by Terry Dugan Design, Minneapolis, Minnesota

AS TIME GOES BY

Published by Harvest House Publishers
Eugene, Oregon 97402

Library of Congress Cataloging-in-Publication Data

Wick, Lori.
As time goes by / Lori Wick.
p. cm.—(The Californians: bk. 2)
ISBN 0-7369-0256-2
I. Title. II. Series: Wick, Lori. Californians: bk 2.
PS 3573.I237A8 1992
813'.54—dc20 91-3144
CIP

Printed in the United States of America.

00 01 02 03 04 /BC/ 7 6 5 4 3 2

I wish to dedicate this book to my sons,

Timothy and Matthew.

Thank you for sledding, ball tag, cartoons in bed,
and times of quiet play, so I'm free to write.
You fill my life with love and joy,
and I praise God that you are mine.

The Taylor and Donovan Families—1871

The Taylor Family

William Taylor
Wife: Mabel (May)
Children:
Jeffrey Taylor
Gilbert Taylor
Nathan Taylor

The Riggs Family

Marshall Riggs
Wife: Kaitlin Donovan Riggs
Extended Family:
Patrick Sean Donovan III
Marcail Donovan

The Bradford Family

Jake Bradford
Wife: Maryanne
Children:
Roberta (Bobbie)
Troy

THE CALIFORNIANS

As Time Goes By

Prologue

Santa Rosa, California
December 1871

Jeffrey Taylor tiptoed up the back stairway of his house in stocking feet. His parents and brothers were all asleep and he stepped carefully along the upstairs hallway to avoid the reliable creaks and groans of the hardwood floor.

Once in his bedroom he lit the lantern and undressed for bed. The sights and sounds from the Christmas party he had just attended came back to him. Jeff knew everyone there, had grown up with most of them. They had laughed, sang, played games, and eaten for hours. And then the hostess' face, Sylvia Weber, swam before his eyes.

"What's the matter with you tonight, Jeff? You haven't been very attentive this evening." Her voice was irritated and Jeff was quick to apologize.

"I'm sorry, I must be a little tired."

"I'll forgive you," Sylvia said with a teasing light in her eyes, "if you come over right now and have one of these desserts I made."

Jeff had gone, telling himself to perk up, but Sylvia was right; he had been distracted the whole evening. It was almost a relief to leave.

He lay in bed now, stretched out flat—almost six feet of him—hands pillowing his head. His body was ready for sleep, but his mind, full of the day's activities and conversations, was moving like a runaway stage. Earlier that day Jeff's father, Bill Taylor, had talked with him. Bill informed Jeff that Jake Bradford had been in to mention that his daughter Roberta was coming back to town and looking for a job.

Roberta Bradford, "Bobbie" to most, was the answer to his parents' prayers because she was an experienced shipping clerk and only needed the position temporarily until she got married.

Jeff had known they were going to be needing someone at the shipping office, owned and operated by the Taylor family, because his mother, May, was taking some time off.

Bill's consultation with Jeff about hiring Roberta was far more than just professional courtesy over the fact that they would all be working together. Bill told Jeff outright that if he didn't want Bobbie to work there, they would drop the whole idea. The reason for such words from father to son dated back five years.

Finally allowing the years in his mind to fall away, Jeff let his thoughts slip back to the summer of 1866, the summer when Jeffrey Taylor's thoughtless actions hurt Bobbie Bradford enough to drive her from her family and home for over five years.

one

Santa Rosa, California
June 1866

Seventeen-year-old Jeff Taylor was not hearing one word of Pastor Keller's sermon. While keeping his head totally still, he could shift his eyes until he had a perfect view of Sylvia Weber's profile. Unfortunately he could also see Richard Black.

How dare Sylvia sit with Richard in church when only last night she had let Jeff hold her hand! The sight of them made Jeff fume, but his anger didn't last. Sylvia smiled at him as soon as church was over, causing his irritation to immediately dissipate.

"We're leaving, Jeff."

The words, spoken by his mother, came much too soon for Jeff's tastes. Why, he had only had a few minutes to talk with his friends and *no* time to speak with Sylvia. She looked wonderful in a pale blue dress shot with flowers of dark blue, the perfect foil for her blonde hair and striking blue eyes.

Jeff wore a brooding look as he climbed into his folks'

wagon. He usually rode with Rigg, his 21-year-old brother, but today Rigg had stayed home with a summer cold.

Actually Rigg was his half-brother—Marshall Riggs. Rigg had been a toddler when his father died and his mother married Bill Taylor. Bill and May had three more boys as the years went on: Jeffrey, Gilbert, who was 13, and Nathan, the youngest at ten.

A huge lunch of fried chicken and dumplings was enough to take Jeff's mind from Sylvia for a few minutes—that and the job his mother had given him of taking some soup up to Rigg. Rigg wasn't really sick enough to stay in bed, but May had wanted him to and he had done so to please her.

"Ready for something to eat?"

"Sure." Rigg put aside his Bible and pushed up in bed. "Smells good."

"Chicken soup."

"How was church?"

"All right."

"You wouldn't know it by your voice."

"Sylvia sat with Richard."

"So it's Sylvia this month." Rigg's voice was dry.

"What's that supposed to mean?"

"Calm down, Jeff." The older man's voice was gentle. "I've just noticed that you don't stay interested in any one girl for very long."

"It's different with Sylvia." Jeff spoke adamantly, a little too adamantly.

Rigg nodded sagely, wisely holding his peace. His food saved him from replying for a few minutes, and then he told Jeff that he needed to get some sleep so he could be at the store in the morning.

Jeff nearly accused Rigg of being married to the store that bore his name—Riggs Mercantile. But the one time he had hinted at such a thing, Rigg gave him quite a tongue-lashing. He told Jeff flat-out that he wouldn't know a day of hard work if it bit him in the seat of the pants.

Jeff had silently agreed with him but replied that these were his fun years. He would have to work the rest of his life, so why start now? Rigg, who had been working at the store since he was 14 and was in complete charge since he was 19, had only shaken his head and walked away.

Jeff consoled himself with the fact that he helped out at the shipping office from time to time. The fact that his ten-year-old and 13-year-old brothers did more work than he did was conveniently ignored as Jeff once again told himself that he would be working the rest of his life. At 17 you were supposed to enjoy life to its fullest.

Jeff was just leaving Rigg's room when his mother called him from the kitchen.

"You have a visitor, Jeffrey."

Certain that Sylvia had come to apologize, Jeff flew down the stairs, only to find Pastor Keller waiting in the living room and talking with his father.

"Hello, Jeff," the pastor greeted him. "Sorry to intrude on your Sunday afternoon, but I have something I'd like to discuss with you."

"Sure." Jeff took a chair and gave the pastor his full attention.

"We're planning an outing for the church. I think everyone will enjoy it. We're going boating at the lagoon."

"Hey, that sounds great!"

"I was hoping you'd say that. We're planning a little something special for the young people, though, and here's where you come in. Right now there are 12 young people from 15 to 17, six boys and six girls. What I'd like to see you do is ask the six boys to invite the girls on this outing. We'll have a picnic and some games before the boating, which isn't scheduled until four in the afternoon. The date is three weeks from today."

Pastor Keller held out a piece of paper to Jeff, who took it and read in silence.

❑❑❑

Jeffrey Taylor	Angie Stallsworth
Tom Freemont	Sylvia Weber
Richard Black	Roberta Bradford
Deacon Briggs	Kimberly Miller
Dan Walton	Dorothy Nelson
Jeremy Reeve	Lydia Caminiti

❑❑❑

"You're one of the older boys, Jeff, and I think a leader. I was hoping you could talk to the other fellows and ask them if they'd be willing to invite a girl from the list."

Pleased at being referred to as a leader, Jeff nodded and continued to listen.

"If you think this is going to make anyone uncomfortable, we'll just drop the asking part and invite the young people as a whole."

"No, this is great," Jeff answered from a purely selfish standpoint, thinking how much fun it would be to attend an event and have Sylvia all to himself. "I'll talk to the others right away and let you know."

"Thanks, Jeff. I knew I could count on you." Pastor Keller took his leave shortly after that and Jeff asked to borrow the wagon. Within two hours all six boys from the list were in the Taylors' yard demolishing a platter of cookies that May had delivered to them.

"So that's the story," Jeff explained. "These are the girls, and Pastor wants us to do the asking."

"Who asks who?" Richard wanted to know.

"That's what we have to decide," Jeff told him without much friendliness in his voice.

"I'll ask Lydia," Jeremy offered, and the other boys, save Jeff and Richard, began to speak up. Within minutes it became apparent that two boys wanted to ask Sylvia and no one wanted to ask Roberta.

"You told Pastor this was a great idea, Jeff; *you* ask four-eyes."

"Hey, Richard, don't talk about Bobbie that way. She's really nice."

"Then you ask her, Deacon," was Richard's surly reply. But Deacon wanted to ask Angie, and being one of the younger boys, he fell silent rather than stand up to Richard, who was almost as old as Jeff.

"It looks like we tell Pastor Keller that it's not going to work out." Jeff voiced his solution even as he told himself that he would just ask Sylvia on his own.

"We could draw straws to see who asks Bobbie Bradford." This was Richard's suggestion, his voice betraying to everyone that he was sure it would never be him. The group fell silent for a moment, and each boy felt weighted down with guilt over the way they were talking about Bobbie.

Deacon was right—Bobbie was a very nice girl but she wasn't at all attractive. She was the youngest girl on the list, not yet 15, and it appeared to anyone who cared to observe that Bobbie was never going to develop any female curves.

She was about as straight up and down as a young girl could be, and even with her short height she appeared to be all arms and legs. Her eyesight was the next thing that weighed on everyone's mind, as each young man pictured the wire-rimmed spectacles she wore on the bridge of her turned-up nose. They made her eyes look like those of an insect, or so the boys thought.

And if those reasons weren't bad enough, Bobbie had the ugliest hair in town. A dirty blonde color, it refused to curl or lay straight, but fluffed out from around Bobbie's head and shoulders like the wool on a sheep.

The Bradford family was not what anyone could call affluent, but Mrs. Bradford was a whiz with a needle and thread, and most people never dreamed that Bobbie wore her mother's made-over dresses. Bobbie had a brother who was 13 and an older married sister, who was expecting her first baby.

The family was well-liked at church and known for their hardworking, generous attitudes. Mr. Bradford did odd jobs around town and was the gravedigger for the church cemetery—not a glamorous position, but appreciated by most. Mrs. Bradford cleaned house for two of Santa Rosa's wealthier families, and had a small business of sewing and mending clothes in her home.

But even though Bobbie's family were hard workers and she was a nice girl, none of the boys in the Taylor yard had the desire to ask her to the outing at the lagoon. The six talked a while longer, and though most of them were overwhelmed with shame, they agreed to draw straws. The fact that this went on in the barn, out of sight from Bill and May Taylor, said much.

Jeff's brother Gilbert wandered into the barn, but he observed from a distance and was not one to talk about anything he had seen or heard.

The youngest boy of the group, Tom Freemont, was elected to hold the straws. Within seconds Jeff stood with the long straw in this hand, trying to control the fury massing inside him.

"Well, that was easy enough," Richard smiled with cruel contentment. "Since we both wanted to ask the same girl, this makes it quite simple."

Jeff forced a smile onto his face. "That settles it all right."

The group dispersed a few minutes later, most of the boys thinking what a good sport Jeff was. Jeff stayed in the barn for a long time trying to calm down. Gil, who had seen the others off and gotten three more cookies, came back into the barn. He flopped into a mound of hay and spoke.

"You should have told Richard to shut up."

"I don't need *you* to tell me what I should have said!"

"You better hope Dad never finds out about those straws."

"Well, he's not going to find out from *me*!" The full import of that statement made Gil come straight up out of the straw. "I never snitch, Jeff!" Gilbert's eyes flashed angry fire and Jeff looked down at his shoes. He knew he should apologize. He wanted to, but Gil stormed out and Jeff was left alone.

Two

"Did all the boys leave?" May asked Jeff as soon as he walked in the kitchen.

"They're gone."

"Did they like the idea?"

"Yeah."

May was bent over a pot on the stove and missed the stormcloud on her son's face.

"How did you work it out? Are you asking Sylvia?"

"No, Richard is asking Sylvia. I'm asking Bobbie Bradford." This announcement was enough to spin May around to face her son.

"Why, Jeffrey!" May exclaimed in delight. "That's wonderful! Bobbie is the sweetest girl on earth." May went back to her cooking with a huge smile on her face.

'Maybe Jeff is growing up after all,' she thought to herself. 'Seventeen is such a *self*-absorbed age. It's nice to see him thinking of someone besides himself for a change.'

May was oblivious to the turmoil going on within her young son. Jeff sat a moment longer deciding what to do. If he went up to his room on a hot Sunday afternoon, his mother would think he was ill. He couldn't go see Rigg because Rigg could read him like a book and would know instantly that something was wrong. If he went to find Gil, and Gil was still mad at him, his parents would want to know what they were quarreling about. Finally, with a small disgruntled sigh, Jeff went into the living room to hide behind a book.

❑❑❑

"I can never beat you in checkers, Bobbie," Angie Stallsworth complained as Bobbie jumped Angie's last two checkers and still had four more of her own on the board.

"That's all right, Angie, you can beat me in spelling any day of the week."

Best friends, the girls were sitting at the Bradford kitchen table on Monday afternoon. School had only been out a month and they were already restless for something to do. Angie had come over wanting Bobbie to go for a walk along the creek, but Bobbie's mother was working and she had strict orders to stay home with her younger brother Troy.

"What'll we do now?" Angie asked.

"Wel-l-l-l," Bobbie drew out the word as she rose silently from the table. "We could head in to town and rob the bank. Gottcha!" Bobbie flung the half-closed door wide open to capture her brother, who was crouched there listening to the girls' conversation.

"Troy Bradford, what were you doing back there?" Bobbie had her brother by the collar and stood looking down at him like an enraged warrior. She let go when she saw how red his face was. He scowled at her for embarrassing him. They apologized to each other and Bobbie spoke quietly.

"Why don't you get a cookie from the tin?"

"Thanks." Troy retrieved his cookie and glanced at Angie before going outside. Bobbie felt sorry for him. She knew he had a crush on Angie. 'But then who wouldn't?' Bobbie thought with a twinge of envy.

Angie was adorable with her dark curly hair and big dark eyes. She had a round little chin and a bright smile. *And* she was developing a figure—something Roberta Jean Bradford was sure would never happen in her own body.

Her mother kept reminding her that she was not yet 15, but Bobbie knew girls who were younger and who had more of a figure than she did. So the words were no comfort.

"Want to bake cookies?" Bobbie suggested.

"It's too hot."

"I guess it is."

"I never thought I'd ever say this, but I miss school."

"Me too." Bobbie agreed. "I miss seeing all the other kids."

"*All* the other kids?" Angie questioned her. "Or just one in particular?"

"Did you see that he was sitting with Sylvia on Sunday?"

"Yeah," Angie said with disgust. "Some guys. I mean, so what if she does have a great face and figure and gets good marks in school? What else has she got?"

Bobbie dissolved into giggles at the comical look on Angie's face. But both girls sobered a moment later; they knew what the other girl didn't have: Sylvia Weber was not a nice person. On more than one occasion Angie or Bobbie had been at the receiving end of her vicious tongue.

"I thought Jeff liked Sylvia," Bobbie commented suddenly.

"I thought so too. At least Jeff and Sylvia deserve each other. He's sorta stuck on himself."

"I've noticed." Bobbie agreed quietly. She didn't like to criticize people, and in fact she went out of her way to say nice things about even the hardest to redeem. "But Jeff is one of the best-looking guys in school."

"That's true. But never forget Bob—all men are fickle."

The girls dissolved once again into shrieks of laughter because Angie herself was in love with a new boy every week.

The afternoon went by in a lazy fashion and the girls ended up playing a game with Troy and having a great time. They parted company just before supper and made plans to meet downtown the next day to browse in the store windows. But Angie was back at the Bradfords' an hour or so before bedtime.

"Hello, Mr. Bradford," Angie said breathlessly when Bobbie's father opened the door. "I need to see Bobbie; can she come out for a minute?"

Bobbie appeared at her father's elbow and Angie nearly dragged her from the house.

"What is the matter with you, Ang?" Bobbie laughed as she was pulled along. Angie stopped under the tree in the yard.

"The church is having an outing at the lagoon and Deacon Briggs just asked me!"

The girls stared at each other for a full five seconds before they screamed in unison and threw their arms around each other.

"I think he's liked you for a long time."

"You do?" Angie's face flushed with pleasure.

"Tell me everything," Bobbie pleaded, and her friend was more than willing to comply.

"We were just finishing supper when he knocked on the door and asked for me. My father made him sit for a few minutes in the parlor and I *know* he was embarrassed. But anyway, we sat on our front porch and he asked if I'd heard there was going to be a boat outing for the whole church."

"The whole church?" Bobbie cut in.

"Yeah, a week from Sunday. But the young people are going early to have a picnic and then boating when everyone arrives."

"Oh, Angie," Bobbie said. "I'm so happy for you. Deacon is one of the nicest boys at church."

"I think so too. He's not stuck on himself, either."

The girls chattered until it was nearly dark and Angie had to go or face trouble at home. Bobbie went back into the house in a dreamy state. Angie's first date. . . . The next best thing to having it happen to *you* was having it happen to your best friend . . . and with Deacon, too, who was so tall and quiet.

Bobbie took great delight in telling her brother about the boat outing, since he usually knew things ahead of her. But when she climbed into bed a short while later her mood wasn't quite so buoyant.

She carefully repeated her nighttime ritual of placing her glasses on the corner of her nightstand. That way she knew where they were even if she was half-asleep. When Bobbie was ten she had once left them on the plant stand in the hall. The glasses afforded her depth perception which she had sorely missed that morning, and she ended up falling all the way down the stairs.

Bobbie rubbed her nose where the spectacles had sat.

It was a relief to remove them, since they had a tendency to pinch.

'I wonder if someone will ask me on a date when I'm 15,' Bobbie wondered as sleep began to crowd in upon her. She fell into slumber visualizing the clothes in Angie's closet so she could tell her tomorrow what she should wear on her date.

three

The boat outing was only four days away when Jeff rode into the Bradfords' yard. They had an old house that they had painted and kept up. The swing that hung from the tree in the yard was just a piece of wood with a rope knotted in the middle.

Troy moved lazily on that swing, pushing himself in circles with one bare toe. As though embarrassed at being caught on the swing at his age, he jumped down the moment he saw Jeff.

"Hi, Troy. Is Bobbie around?"

"In the kitchen."

Jeff tied the horse's reins to a tree limb and moved toward the house in his long-legged stride. His knock on the door went unanswered, and for an instant he entertained the idea of leaving without seeing Bobbie.

"Just go in," Troy called from where he had sat down under the tree. Jeff glanced at the younger boy, hesitated, and opened the door. He found himself in the living room.

"Bobbie." His voice was hesitant and soft.

"Bobbie." Louder this time. Jeff heard someone move in the next room, and then Bobbie came out drying her hands on a towel.

"Well, hello, Jeff, how are you?" Bobbie greeted him with natural ease, smiling the smile that came so easily for her.

"I'm fine, thank you." Jeff sounded too formal, even to his own ears.

"My folks aren't here right now, but I can give them a message if you'd like." It never once occurred to Bobbie that Jeff was there to see *her*. She also knew that Troy was in the yard, and that if Jeff had wanted him he would never have come in the house. Her parents were the only ones left.

"I'm not here to see your folks."

"Oh." Bobbie took a moment to absorb this. "Why don't you come in to the kitchen? I've got cookies ready to come out of the oven." Bobbie turned and walked away, taking for granted that Jeff would follow.

Jeff took a chair at the kitchen table and glanced around the Bradfords' kitchen. It was spacious and sparkling clean, but Jeff didn't really notice amid his reluctance to be there. A moment later Bobbie set a hot pan of cookies on the table.

"Help yourself, Jeff. I'll get you something to drink."

Jeff thought the cookies might take his mind off the inevitable, so he picked one up and bit into it. It was delicious.

"I hope you like cider," Bobbie said as she set a cup before her guest and took a seat.

A moment passed before Jeff saw that Bobbie was waiting peacefully for him to state his business. He said the first thing that came to mind.

"These cookies are good." He sounded so surprised that Bobbie smiled.

"Thank you. Have as many as you like."

"Thanks." Jeff ate a few more.

Bobbie continued to wait quietly, but began to feel distinctly uncomfortable. She didn't really know Jeff Taylor and couldn't think for the life of her why he would come to see her. He suddenly cleared his throat and spoke.

"I suppose you've heard about the outing at the lagoon."

"Yes, I heard."

"Well, I came by today to ask you if you'd like to go with me."

Jeff watched the eyes behind those glasses blink at him even as he prayed she'd say no. It wasn't that he found her repulsive, because Deacon was right, she was very nice. But he was sure that if Sylvia saw him with Bobbie he would never hear the end of it—not to mention the fact that he didn't want to do anything to ruin the fragile thread upon which their relationship hung.

"I'd like that, Jeff. Thank you for asking me."

"Sure."

"Is there anything I can bring?" Jeff, becoming more relaxed by the second, bit into another cookie before he answered.

"No, I don't think so. Oh, I'll be picking you up early. You see, we're going to have a picnic and some games, then everyone else will come at 4:00 and we'll all go boating."

"That sounds fine. If you find out I need to bring something, just let me know."

"Okay." Jeff stood on that word and reached for another cookie. "These are really very good."

"I'm glad you think so. I was a little worried because you only ate seven of them."

Jeff's head whipped back as he was walking away from her. She was actually teasing him! Her eyes sparkled with mirth and a small smile played around the corners of her mouth.

If Jeff had taken the time to really look, he would have noticed the beautiful green color of Bobbie's eyes and how given her pretty mouth was to smiling.

Jeff's own mouth raised in a small smile and he thanked Bobbie for the cider and cookies.

"I'll see you Sunday," Bobbie called to him as he rode out of the yard. Jeff waved and Bobbie walked back into the kitchen and plopped into a chair.

"Jeffrey Taylor just invited me out." Bobbie hoped it would seem more real to her if she heard the words aloud, but it didn't. She continued to sit almost in a daze. Troy came in and finished eating the pan of cookies Jeff started, but she didn't notice.

Bobbie was thinking back two years in time, to the fall and the first day of school. They had not attended the same church as the Taylors in those days, and so Bobbie had not seen Jeff over the summer.

She couldn't believe how tall he had grown over the summer months, and neither could most of the other girls. He became the object of so much attention in the first few weeks that he began to change. He had never been mean or vicious, but suddenly he went from open and friendly to aloof and unapproachable.

The *old* Jeff had shown kindness to Bobbie on more than one occasion, even defending her when she was teased about her eyesight. Now he stayed quiet if the older kids made unkind remarks, or he just behaved as though she didn't exist. Any little infatuations Bobbie had for Jeff had been slowly crushed beneath the heels of his indifference.

And now he had just come over and asked her to the boat outing. Bobbie was thrilled. Her open, honest approach to life made her somewhat naive to the underhanded ways and thought processes of some people. It never even occurred to her that Jeff had asked her for any other reason than the fact he wanted to spend the day with her.

"Roberta!" Maryanne Bradford's outraged voice broke through Bobbie's dream world. "You're burning the cookies!"

"Oh no, I'm sorry, Mom." The women reached simultaneously for the oven pad to rescue the burning pan but Maryanne ended up doing the work.

"Honestly, Bobbie, it wasn't as if you weren't sitting right here," her mother said in some exasperation.

"I know and I'm sorry, but Mom, the most wonderful thing just happened. Jeff Taylor came by and asked me to the boat outing on Sunday!"

"He did?" Maryanne said with a smile.

"I can go, can't I? I know I'm not 15 yet, but Daddy will say yes, won't he?" Maryanne looked into her daughter's eyes, so full of hopeful entreaty, and smiled.

"Jeff is a nice young man. Of course he'll say yes."

"Oh thanks, Mom, thanks!" Bobbie threw her arms around her mother and squeezed her tight. Then she broke away suddenly, her face showing her horror.

"Mother! What will I wear?" Maryanne watched her daughter flap her hands in a state of panic and then charge for the stairs. She was back down before she had gone five steps.

"Angie! I've got to tell Angie!" This time she watched Bobbie fly out the front door running as fast as she could.

"What's her problem?" Troy asked his mother, who was standing at the door still watching her daughter run.

"Bobbie needs to tell Angie something. No problem really."

"Well, whatever it was, it made her burn the cookies. I can smell 'em out here." Troy made no effort to masquerade his disgust.

"Well, I wouldn't worry about it, dear, since you've never let singed edges stop you before."

"No, I guess I haven't." Troy slipped past his mother and into the house. Maryanne followed a few minutes later, joining Troy in the kitchen. She emptied the contents of her purse onto the table and began to count, praying as she did that she would have enough for a surprise for her daughter.

four

Maryanne Bradford went a little out of her way as she walked home the next day after work. She had left that morning feeling regretful over not having enough money to buy fabric for a new dress for Bobbie. She wished they had had more notice; then she could have put a little aside over a few weeks.

But then Mrs. Walcott, the lady for whom she cleaned two mornings a week, had asked her to do a few additional things, and Maryanne had been paid extra. It was still going to make things a little tight until next week, but they would get by; they always did.

Maryanne walked into Riggs Mercantile and headed straight to the fabric counter. She had priced and fingered several bolts when someone spoke behind her.

"Hello, Maryanne."

"Hi, May, I didn't even see you."

"I was upstairs talking with Rigg. Are you looking for fabric?"

"Yes, I'm sure you know that Jeff asked our Bobbie to the lagoon outing, and I want to surprise her with a new dress."

May smiled. "I almost asked how you could have it done in time, and then I remembered I was talking with Maryanne Bradford."

Maryanne beamed over the compliment and asked May what she thought of a certain piece of cotton. The background was a jade green with a pattern of tiny white flowers.

"Bobbie's eyes are green, aren't they?"

"Yes."

"Oh, this will be perfect."

"I emptied my purse last night to see if we could afford this, and then had to ask the Lord to help me accept the fact that we couldn't. Then today I got paid a little extra. If we're careful until next week, Bobbie should have her dress. I usually cut my own dresses down for her and she never complains, but I can't wait to see her face when she finds out she'll have a dress from *new* cloth."

"There's something inside us, isn't there, Maryanne, that yearns for our children to have all they need and a little more?"

"Isn't that the truth! Don't get me wrong, May, I'm not hearing wedding bells or anything, but you wouldn't have believed the look on Bobbie's face when she told me Jeff asked her. It was a mixture of excitement and fear all rolled into one."

"I know they'll have a good time." May touched Maryanne's arm and then said she had to be on her way. Maryanne took the fabric to the front and started home again in a few moments.

Bobbie had started supper and was up to her elbows in a flour mixture for fried chicken. Maryanne made her wash her hands and sit at the table.

"But, Mom, I'll just get them all messy again when I pick up the chicken."

"I know, but for the moment you need clean hands. Now close your eyes." Bobbie's brows lowered for a moment, but then she did as she was told.

Maryanne popped into the living room to retrieve a small parcel wrapped in plain brown paper. Her husband, Jake, came in the front door at that instant and Maryanne signaled him over.

"All right, now you can open your eyes and the package." Mother and Father stood silently by as their daughter tore the paper back to reveal the most beautiful fabric she said she had ever seen.

"It's for you—for a new dress to wear on Sunday afternoon."

"Oh Mom, Dad!" Bobbie breathed as she smoothed the wonderful material with her hands. She missed the meaningful glance exchanged between the adults.

"I'll explain later," Maryanne whispered softly as Jake put his arm around his wife. They had discussed it the night before and Jake had been as regretful as Maryanne over Bobbie not having a new dress.

The women went to work right after supper and Bobbie was so excited she could barely hold still. The dress was finished by lunch the next day and all she could do was stand in front of the mirror in her parents' room and look at herself.

Bobbie thought her mother had to be the most clever seamstress in all the world. The dress bloused out at the waist, which gave hint to a fuller chest than there actually was. The sleeves were short and puffed and the neckline was high. The fullness at the waist also made Bobbie's hips more attractive for a change and not just skinny.

"I take it you're pleased."

"Oh Daddy, didn't she do a wonderful job?"

"She always does."

"Do you think Jeff will like it?"

"How could he not?" Her father said with a smile, and Bobbie turned back to the mirror with her eyes shining.

'How could he not?' She repeated to herself. 'How could he not?'

❑❑❑

Jeff and his date were the last to arrive at the lagoon. Bobbie noticed the change in Jeff from the wagon ride over, where he had been fairly talkative, to when they joined the other young people and he had grown very quiet. She didn't understand it or question him, though she wanted to.

"Hi, Jeff; hi, Bobbie." Pastor Keller's wife greeted them as they came toward the blankets spread with a picnic lunch. The day was beautiful, with a slight breeze, and there was plenty of shade under the huge willow trees.

Bobbie and Jeff ended up next to Angie and Deacon on the edge of the blanket. The girls immediately began to visit, and within seconds Deacon joined them. It didn't immediately register with any of them that Jeff was playing with a blade of grass, not looking or talking to anyone.

He perked up a bit when they ate, but the fact that Richard and Sylvia were right across from him was almost more than he could take. He told himself not to look at Sylvia, but he did, again and again. Each time her eyes challenged him in a way that should have made him angry but instead just made him want to be with her all the more. Jeff also found it very satisfying that Richard himself noticed how often Sylvia looked across the blanket.

After lunch they played a few games. The Kellers had more planned but nearly everyone said they wanted to sit and talk. Couples sat together at a distance or small groups visited and laughed in the sun.

Jeff and Bobbie ended up back by the picnic lunch, where Bobbie watched Jeff watching Sylvia. She was more confused than hurt. If Jeff had wanted to ask Sylvia, why didn't he? Bobbie didn't believe that he had asked and been turned down, not with the way she had been looking back all afternoon.

"Would you rather we joined one of the other couples, Jeff?" Bobbie asked solicitously. Everyone else was in sight and Bobbie so much wanted to enjoy the day. But if Jeff kept this up it was going to be miserable.

"No, I like it here under the trees." Jeff had finally looked at Bobbie when she spoke to him, and for the first time he caught a very vulnerable look on her face. He told himself he was being unfair to her, so he turned his whole body to face her, also making it impossible to see Richard and Sylvia.

"I like it under the trees too."

"Is this a new dress?" Jeff was hoping it was, since he had never paid any attention to what Bobbie was wearing before. He wouldn't have known if she had worn it once or a hundred times.

"Yes. My mother made it for me."

"It's nice."

"Thanks. Do you want a carrot stick?" The basket was lying near and Bobbie offered it to Jeff after taking a stick for herself.

"No, thanks." Jeff's mind was wandering again. He wasn't looking at Sylvia but he wasn't talking to Bobbie either.

"I'm glad Troy isn't here."

"Why's that?" Jeff asked, thinking he really didn't care.

"He always puts carrot sticks up his nose."

"Well, kids will do that," Jeff answered noncommittally without even looking at Bobbie.

"Of course it isn't any wonder. My mother does it all the time."

Jeff looked sharply at the small girl beside him to see she was barely containing her laughter. His mouth dropped open when she spoke next because her voice was dripping with sarcasm.

"Very good, Jeffrey. You were actually listening." Bobbie grinned at him and Jeff found himself laughing hard.

"You," he said as he shook a finger at Bobbie, "are incredibly sassy."

"So I've been told," Bobbie admitted without apology. "But at least I don't put carrots in my nose."

"You know," Jeff said thoughtfully, feeling fully relaxed for the first time, "it might be kind of fun." He raised a carrot stick toward his face and Bobbie laughingly snatched it away from him.

"You have very nice teeth, did you know that?" Jeff asked Bobbie suddenly, and she looked surprised and then very serious.

"Is it really so important, Jeff, to be with someone good-looking? I mean, do good looks mean that much to you that you need to find something about me that's attractive?" Bobbie could see that she had shocked him, but she kept her eyes on his and could tell he was thinking.

"I think you're right. I do put too much stock on good looks. If I hurt you just then, I'm sorry."

"Oh, don't apologize Jeff, or feel bad." Bobbie's voice grew dry, but her eyes were sparkling. "You're just a teenage boy and they usually don't know any better."

Jeff looked shocked again, and then let his head fall back against the tree and laughed—a deep-down laugh that came from the pit of his stomach and nearly made it ache.

They talked undisturbed for the next half-hour. Jeff couldn't believe what a good time he was having. Roberta Bradford was a lot of fun. He had even managed to forget Sylvia, until he looked up to see her and Richard headed their way.

"My, but there's a lot of laughter going on over here." Sylvia's mouth was smiling but her eyes weren't.

"Yeah, Jeff, how's the long straw?"

Jeff leveled Richard with a look that was almost dangerous. The other boy knew he had overstepped his bounds and immediately shut his mouth. Sylvia wasn't so tactful.

"Oh, come now, Jeff. Don't get so mad. I'm sure Bobbie understands that you wouldn't have brought her if you'd had a choice."

Once again Jeff's furious eyes were directed at Richard, now knowing that he had told Sylvia what they had done in the barn. Jeff then looked to the young woman with whom he believed himself to be in love. She had never had Jeff angry with her before, and it was almost frightening. When Richard pulled on her hand she left the other couple willingly. No one noticed that Bobbie's face had lost all color.

"What did Richard mean, Jeff?" Bobbie asked softly.

"It's nothing, Bobbie. Forget it."

"That's not true, Jeff, or you'd be looking me in the eye."

Jeff didn't answer, and Bobbie heard Richard's words again in her mind: "The long straw."

"You drew straws to see who would ask me, didn't you, Jeff?" Two other couples were close now, and when Jeff still wouldn't look at her, Bobbie's eyes traveled to the others.

'They all know,' she realized in an instant as their eyes regarded her with embarrassment and pity.

"I'm not feeling very well, Jeff. I'd really like it if you'd take me home."

"We haven't gone boating yet," Jeff said almost desperately, seeing how quickly the afternoon was about to be ruined. "See, all the boats are stacked over there waiting. All the families will be arriving in about a half-hour."

"You're welcome to come back and go boating, Jeff, but the truth is, I'm not feeling so well. I want to go home."

When Jeff made no move to comply, Bobbie turned and walked away from him. It took a moment before he could see she was going to walk home. He ran and stopped her with a hand on her arm.

"Bobbie, do you really want to leave?"

"Did you really draw straws or am I jumping to conclusions?"

"We drew straws." The words were fraught with shame.

"For all the girls or just me?"

Jeff swallowed convulsively. "Just you."

"Please take me home."

Jeff nodded. "Wait here while I hitch the horses."

Bobbie stood stock-still as Jeff went to get the wagon and to tell Pastor they were leaving. She didn't even acknowledge Angie when she called to her. She climbed into the wagon as soon as Jeff stopped beside her, even before he could help her.

On the ride home the silence became oppressive. Jeff didn't know what to say. Sorry wasn't enough. He found himself begging God to turn back the hands of time and let him live the last three weeks over; he promised he would do better.

There was no one home at the Bradfords. Bobbie told Jeff goodbye and went inside. Jeff sat in the wagon for a time, not sure whether to head home or to the lagoon. He finally opted for home. He knew he was going to be in more trouble than he had ever been in his life. But even if he was waiting to kill him, Jeff Taylor had to see his father.

five

"Jeff, how could you?" The question came from his mother and her faced mirrored the torment within. "Maryanne Bradford bought dress material with money she didn't have to make this day special! I don't even know why I said that, Jeff; no one should receive the treatment that you gave Bobbie!"

Jeff didn't respond. He stood by the fireplace and let his mother's angry voice rain down on him.

It hadn't taken very long for the story to circulate among the group at the lagoon, which didn't say much for the congregation's ability to refrain from gossip. Understandably, neither the Taylors nor the Bradfords stayed for the boating.

Jeff had not waited long for his family to arrive back at the house. Gilbert and Nathan had discreetly disappeared and Jeff faced his parents alone. Bill said nothing as May berated her son.

"Your actions of the past weeks make perfect sense now—your waiting until the last minute to ask Bobbie and then doing so as though you were going to your own hanging." May continued to point out Jeff's faults, ending with the fact that he had deceived everyone, not just Bobbie. A moment later a look of silent communication passed between husband and wife and May exited the room.

"Sit down, Jeff," Bill said, once his wife was gone. Jeff sat on the sofa but could not get comfortable. He shifted several times even as his father pulled the rocker close in front of him.

"I want you to tell me everything."

Jeff did just that, beginning with the boys' conversation in the yard and the drawing of straws in the barn, to the moment he dropped Bobbie at her house and came directly home himself.

"You mean to tell me that Richard and Sylvia came right up to you and Bobbie and called her the 'long straw'?" Bill's voice reflected his amazement.

Jeff's eyes filled with tears and his shoulders began to shake. "You should have seen her face, Dad; she was crushed. And it's all my fault. I wanted to have Sylvia all to myself and I was willing to do anything—" Jeff's voice broke and he began to sob in earnest.

Bill joined him on the couch, and with his arm around his errant son, he listened as Jeff shared everything he was feeling and cried himself into near-exhaustion.

They talked for the better part of two hours and then prayed together. Jeff confessed his selfish, deceitful actions and then listened in surprise as Bill confessed his lack of attention to his oldest biological son. Bill went on to pray for wisdom for Jeff when he apologized to Bobbie and her family as well as wisdom for himself when he went to see Richard and then Sylvia. Father and son were more than a little drained at the end of the prayer.

"Do you think I should go tonight?"

"No, son, I think you need to get some rest. You can see Bobbie in the morning."

"Thanks, Dad."

"I love you, Jeff." The men embraced and then Jeff took himself off to bed. He was up early, but not being sure when the Bradfords would be up and about, he waited until 8:30 to go over. When he arrived, a sober Mr. Bradford informed him that Bobbie had left on the morning stage. She planned to visit her aunt and uncle for the remainder of the summer.

six

Jenner, California
January 2, 1872

"Have you got everything?"

"Yes, Aunt Joanne, I've got everything." Roberta Bradford uttered the words indulgently; it was the fifth time she had been asked.

"Oh honey," the older woman cried softly, and hugged Bobbie to herself. "What are we going to do without you?"

"You'll be fine."

"Is it wrong for me to pray that Cleve convinces you?"

Bobbie opened her mouth to say something but closed it again; she wasn't sure she wanted to touch that one. Thankful that Cleveland Ramsey had not come to see her off, Bobbie turned away from her aunt to face her Uncle Jasper. He was a replica of her father both in looks and personality, a quiet rock of support. But today he had tears in his eyes. Seeing them, Bobbie's own tears came very close to the surface.

"What can I say?" Bobbie said softly. Her uncle shook his head and enfolded her in his arms.

The stage pulled in a few minutes later and Bobbie's bags were thrown into the back. She gave her beloved aunt and uncle one last hug and this time the tears could not be stemmed. She waved from the stage window, her eyes still streaming as the stage pulled away.

Bobbie was thankful she had the interior to herself. She allowed herself a good cry and then let her head fall back against the seat, her thoughts drifting to the past and then jumping to the future in rapid succession.

Five years. She had actually been away from home for over five years. It didn't feel that long, not while it was passing, and not even now that it was over.

There had been talk over those years of her returning to Santa Rosa, but the plans were always delayed. At one point when she had been away three years, her parents had decided it was time she come home, but Uncle Jasper had fallen ill, making her presence at the shipping office crucial. No matter how many times she asked herself how the years had slipped by, no answer came. She really loved living in Jenner and she had been so young when she left Santa Rosa—a little girl in so many ways.

But she wasn't a little girl now. She was a woman, headed back to take a job at the Taylors' office—a job she could walk into with confidence because of her experience. Bobbie knew her aunt and uncle's shipping office was nowhere near as busy as the Taylors' in Santa Rosa, but she knew the routine, how to handle packages and treat the customers as well.

And she would be working with the Taylors. Mr. Taylor had given a full explanation as to why they needed her. Business had picked up to the point that May needed a rest. Bobbie was to take her place and her fellow employees would be Jeff, Gilbert, and sometimes Nate.

Jeff. A myriad of emotions flooded through Bobbie at the thought of Jeffrey Taylor, but none were anger or bitterness. They'd had no contact over the years except one note; Bobbie still had it. She had received it in the fall after that awful summer when he had obviously understood that she was not coming back for the next school year. It had been very brief, four short words, but they had meant the world to her: "I'm sorry, Bobbie, Jeff."

She hadn't replied and it hadn't changed the hurt, but it helped to know that he regretted the way he had treated her. At the time she received it, she hoped he was suffering too. But the next summer all of that changed when, for the first time, Bobbie truly listened to the man who was preaching at the front of the church she was in and Bobbie understood that she was a sinner.

When she was very young the man in the pulpit had never taught anything but God's love. And then the Bradford family started attending Pastor Keller's church and he had the courage to tell people that they must be born again, that without the saving blood of Jesus Christ they would not live forever with God. But Bobbie hadn't believed Pastor Keller.

She agreed with her first pastor, a man whose name she couldn't even remember, that God was a God of love. She didn't believe He would ever send anyone good to hell. And then it became very clear to Bobbie as she studied the Bible that God didn't send anyone to hell. It was man's choice, *her choice—Roberta Bradford's*—as to where she spent her eternity.

With Bobbie's belief in Jesus Christ came a new outlook on everything, especially the way she had been treated at the lagoon. The weight of bitterness was lifted from Bobbie as she studied the Word of God with her aunt and uncle. As she did, she learned that there was no room for unforgiveness in the heart of a Christian who desired to serve God with her whole heart.

Bobbie's drifting thoughts were interrupted again and again as the stage stopped and other passengers boarded or disembarked. It was well into the evening when a very tired young woman finally arrived in Santa Rosa. It felt wonderful to stretch her legs. As Bobbie set out on the walk home, she was also thankful that the skies were clear. Her fatigue fell away as she passed well-known sights—the post office, Riggs Mercantile, the barber shop—each one familiar and beloved even in the rapidly descending darkness.

Spotting her house, Bobbie began to run. Her parents were not expecting her for two more days, but they wouldn't be sorry to see her now. Bobbie stopped just short of throwing open the door. Drawing in a deep breath, she put her bags down. She rapped hard and stood still, telling herself to breathe as she waited.

Maryanne, never dreaming her daughter would arrive early, wished she had brought a lantern with her to the door so she could see who was on her front step.

"Who is it, Mary?" Jake called from somewhere in the living room.

"Tell him it's Bobbie," Bobbie said softly before her mother could make a sound, and then Bobbie watched her mother dissolve into tears. She didn't move to touch her daughter or try to speak to her; she couldn't. She cried uncontrollably in a way that she hadn't for over five years.

Jake came on the scene to find his daughter's arms around his wife, attempting to comfort her and stop her tears. Jake added his own tears as his arms went around both of his girls, and the three of them stood still, no one noticing the cold air coming in from the open door.

"Mom, try to stop," Bobbie pleaded.

"Come and sit down, Mary." Jake led his wife to the sofa and sat on one side of her. Bobbie quickly retrieved her bags from the porch and closed the front door. Not noticing that the house looked wonderful, her attention was centered wholly on her distraught mother.

"I'm sorry, Mom, I shouldn't have surprised you," Bobbie said as she sat on the sofa next to her mother. The words were like cold water in the face of the distressed woman.

"Oh Bobbie, no," she choked out. "I'm just so glad to see you and it's been so long." She cried some more but was finally gaining some control. Bobbie glanced over to see her father grinning at her. She smiled back.

"Welcome home."

"Thanks." Bobbie's smile nearly stretched off her face.

"Stand up and let me look at you." Bobbie complied and stood quietly for his inspection.

"Have I changed?" Bobbie asked the question with exaggerated innocence and her father chuckled.

"You're not much taller but there's definitely more to you." Jake Bradford's eyes sparkled and it was Bobbie's turn to chuckle.

"Well, I got my wish and finally developed in the front but the Lord was overly generous in the back." Bobbie's voice was dry.

Jake laughed in earnest then. The Bradford women were notorious for having smaller bustlines and larger posteriors.

"Don't you fret, Bobbie. You've got a nice figure, just like your mother's, and she's got a great—"

"Jacob!" Maryanne spoke sharply, and both husband and daughter laughed. Maryanne patted the sofa and

Bobbie sat on the edge, turning to face her mother, who lay back against the cushions.

"Look at you," she breathed as she gazed into her daughter's face. "Why didn't we ever think to cut your hair? Just look at those dark blonde curls," Maryanne said with a small shake of her head. Bobbie only shrugged and smiled.

In truth her hair was darling, cut short all around her head and so curly. It was a natural curl that simply hadn't had a chance against the weight of Bobbie's previous longer style. The frames on Bobbie's glasses were a little different now, but other than the hair and glasses, she was very much the same. Her mouth still smiled just as easily and her eyes were still a beautiful deep green.

"Where's Troy?" Bobbie asked quickly when it looked as though her mother would cry again.

"On a date."

Bobbie's parents took great delight over the way their daughter's mouth dropped open.

"A date?"

"That's right. He'll be home pretty soon."

"Why didn't anyone mention this in their letters?"

"It just happened," Jake informed her with a smile.

Bobbie had a thousand questions then, and before her parents could answer them all, Troy walked in. He was a good six inches taller than she was and even had a mustache. Bobbie could only stare at her 18-year-old brother. Troy stared back.

"Hi, Bobbie," the young man finally said, his voice as deep as Jake's.

"Hi, brat," Bobbie said fondly. Another moment passed and then Troy grabbed her and squeezed her tight. They laughed and talked nonstop for the next hour before

Bobbie told her family she was going to be too tired to walk the stairs if she didn't go to bed.

"Have you told her about our plans for the weekend?" Troy said softly as his sister started out of the room.

"No," Jake said when he was sure she couldn't hear. "I thought I'd surprise her over breakfast."

The three remaining in the living room shared a conspiratorial grin and then sat in silence and listened to the floor creak above them as Bobbie readied for bed. Maryanne couldn't remember when anything sounded so sweet.

seven

"It's about time you got up." Bobbie was greeted by her brother's voice and she smiled sleepily at him.

"I'd forgotten how soft that bed was," Bobbie commented as she poured herself a cup of coffee and joined him at the kitchen table. "Where is everyone?"

"Dad's working and Mom ran uptown. She thought you might want to go but decided to let you sleep."

Bobbie moved from the table and began to fix herself some breakfast. She had eggs in the pan when she asked Troy a question that had been on her mind since last night.

"So tell me, Troy, how long have you been seeing Carla Johnson?"

"Yesterday was the third time."

"Where do you and Carla usually go?"

"Last night her folks asked me to supper and then we played a game. The times before that we just went for a walk."

Bobbie grinned and they continued to talk. There wasn't really much catching up to do, since they had all kept as close as the mail would allow.

"Did Cleve see you off?" Troy asked.

"No, just Uncle Jasper and Aunt Joanne. I'm kind of glad he didn't."

"You're not sure, are you? I mean, nothing is definite?"

"No, it's not. Cleveland is a wonderful man and we care for each other, but marriage is such a big step. I hate the idea of living away from Santa Rosa the rest of my life. Now tell me something, Troy—if I desperately wanted to marry Cleve, would it matter to me where I lived?"

Troy's brows rose. "I see your point."

As they discussed the matter Bobbie suddenly noticed a pair of her brother's jeans lying on the table next to the newspaper.

"I take it these need mending."

"They might after you put them on."

"What is that supposed to mean?" Bobbie's voice was indignant.

"Only that you probably won't fit as easily into my jeans as you once did for our camping trips."

"We're going camping?" Bobbie whispered, her voice and face radiating excitement.

"That's the plan." Troy answered her calmly, but inside he was as excited as his sister.

"When do we leave?"

"Since you don't have to be to work until Monday, we'll head out Friday afternoon and come back sometime Sunday."

Bobbie wanted to jump around the kitchen like a kid out of school. How she had missed the camping trips with her dad and brother! They continued to discuss the camping trip and then Troy said he had to leave for work.

Enjoying the feel of home once again, Bobbie stayed at the kitchen table for a long time. Her thoughts wandered and then centered on her family, primarily her sister Alice.

Alice had been pregnant when Bobbie left for Jenner and surprised everyone with twins. The twins had just turned five and Bobbie had never seen them, something she planned on changing that very afternoon.

Maryanne came in a short time later, and mother and daughter sat over coffee and talked like old friends.

"How is your Aunt Joanne?"

"When I left she was crying but she's doing well. I know she hopes I'll be back before the summer is out, as Mrs. Cleveland Ramsey."

"And what do you hope?" Maryanne inquired of her daughter.

"That Cleve will suddenly want to move to Santa Rosa."

"That would make him the perfect husband?"

"Not perfect, I guess, but certainly more appealing. And like I said to Troy, if I was wild to marry Cleve, would it matter where we lived?"

"You might find that you feel differently in a few months, honey; you might find you don't really want to stay in Santa Rosa after all." Bobbie stared at her mother in surprise.

"Don't get me wrong, Bobbie," she explained. "I wish we could live out the rest of our lives living only a few blocks from each other, but I must face facts. Santa Rosa has changed in five years, and so have you. And you might miss Cleve so much that the miles between us won't seem near so important. As hard as it would be to see you go, I would understand. I feel God has been preparing me for something just like this for a long time."

"Oh Mom," Bobbie spoke as she hugged her. "I missed you so much."

Maryanne couldn't stop the tears as her own arms surrounded her daughter. They were probably closer through letters than they might have been if Bobbie had lived at home during her transitional teenage years, but it didn't stop the ache. It didn't ease the longing of wanting to touch and hug each other for all those years and not be able. Who would have thought five years would pass?

"Look at us," Bobbie said as she wiped her streaming face. "We really have got to stop getting each other wet. Now," Bobbie continued with determination, "I want to go see Alice and the kids. Do you want to come?"

"Sure. I just have a few things to do and then we can start. Do you need to stop at the shipping office?"

"No. When I wrote back to Mr. Taylor and accepted the job, he said that unless he heard otherwise he'd plan on my starting work the morning of the eighth."

"Good enough." Maryanne moved from the table to do a few things, and a half-hour later the women were headed to the other side of town. They had a mile walk ahead of them to the Townsend residence.

Alice Bradford had married Stuart Townsend the summer after she finished school. He was four years older and she had met him when attending a party on the far side of Santa Rosa. For Stuart, seeing Alice was love at first sight.

Alice was very shy, even where her family was concerned, and had been slightly overwhelmed by the attention of this stranger. She was not yet done with school, and she knew Stuart to be a man with his own room in one of the boarding houses *and* a steady job at the bank. Stuart was relentless, however, and by the time Alice completed her final year he had won her heart.

Stuart adored his wife and was crazy about his children. In fact he was so tender that he had insisted that Alice go to visit Bobbie when she had been gone for over two years. Maryanne had wanted to go in the worst way, but both of the ladies she cleaned for had planned parties and would not have been prepared to let her off for several weeks.

Maryanne and Bobbie walked the distance in companionable conversation. They were both dressed warmly, since January in Santa Rosa is usually rainy and quite cool, enough to chill a person to the bone if not dressed appropriately.

Alice's home was a welcome sight at the end of their journey, and the sisters embraced for long moments. Alice was much the same, and even though she was not talkative, her expression told her sister how glad she was to have her back.

They settled in the kitchen and Alice set mugs of coffee in front of her sister and mother. A moment later Paige and Wesley entered the room. They stood shyly near their mother at the stove as they greeted their grandmother, and then, seeing their Aunt Bobbie for the first time, they stared in wide-eyed silence.

"Hello," Bobbie said softly, and told herself she was not going to cry. Paige and Wesley Townsend were adorable. They were both blonde and freckled and their eyes were the exact shade of green as her own. Alice had dressed them warmly and in matching outfits. Wesley's pants were the same material as Paige's jumper, a heavy brown corduroy, and their shirts, a brown-and-red plaid, also matched.

Alice had been dressing them alike since the day they were born. Once, when the twins were four, she had mentioned buying fabrics that were different. The twins reacted with such vehement protests to this suggestion that Alice had dropped the whole idea.

Bobbie knew how easy it would be to overreact and throw her arms around these dear children, to whom she was an absolute stranger. They, on the other hand, were as familiar to her as they could be. Everyone, Troy included, had something to say about them in every letter—not to mention Alice's letters, in which she talked about little else.

The five-year-olds watched Bobbie reach for her bag. She brought forth a pair of blue mittens and a pair of red. Next she drew out an orange stick of candy which joined the blue mittens and a red stick to go with the other pair. And finally a red ribbon joined the pile of red items, all intended for Paige. A whistle carved from wood was set next to the blue mittens and orange candy, which were to go to Wesley.

"These are for you, Paige," Bobbie said as she pushed the red pile a little closer to the edge of the table. "And these," Bobbie said as she repeated the movement with the other things, "are for you, Wes."

"What do you say to your Aunt Bobbie?" Alice asked softly.

"Thank you, Aunt Bobbie," the children chorused in voices equally as soft. Bobbie's eyes filled with tears and she busied herself with her coffee to hide the fact.

The children came forward and stood next to their gifts. Bobbie, so wanting to get off to a good start with these little ones, did not immediately look at them.

When she did, she found them both grinning at her. Bobbie smiled back with such delight that they both began to talk at once.

Within ten minutes Paige was in her lap and Wesley was sitting with his grandmother. It never once occurred to Bobbie that her family would talk to these children about her. Why, they knew everything!

"What do you look like without your glasses?" Wes wanted to know. Bobbie removed her spectacles and awaited their inspection.

"She looks the same," Paige stated calmly—"real pretty."

Bobbie hugged the little girl to herself and was surprised a moment later when Alice asked what they wanted for lunch. She couldn't believe how the morning had flown.

When Maryanne and Bobbie finally left, Bobbie was buoyant. She couldn't stop talking about her wonderful niece and nephew.

"Oh Mom, I've just had a terrific idea. Do you suppose Dad would let Paige and Wes go camping with us?"

"Oh Bobbie, I don't know."

"Well, I could at least ask. I mean, it's three adults and only two children; we outnumber them and I can tell what good kids they are."

"Oh Bob, I don't know," Maryanne repeated, and her daughter laughed.

"You're such a worrier, Mom. I'm sure Dad will say yes, not to mention Troy. He'll love the idea."

Maryanne didn't look the least bit convinced, but kept silent. This was one she was more than willing to let Jake handle.

eight

"I know Alice will say yes if you talk to her, Dad. Tell her they can sleep with me. You know how warm we'll all be."

Jake Bradford regarded his daughter and tried not to laugh. She was 14 all over again as they discussed the camping trip. She had nearly leaped on him and Troy when they came in the front door for supper with her idea of taking Paige and Wesley with them.

Troy and Jake had exchanged a quick look; they had honestly never considered it. They also thought it was a great idea, but they weren't about to let Bobbie know that, at least not yet.

"They're pretty young, Bobbie," Troy said skeptically, his eyes just beginning to sparkle.

"We were younger the first time Dad took us," Bobbie pointed out logically, and for the first time noticed that her family was enjoying this.

"Well, maybe you're right," Bobbie went on with a show of disappointment that could have convinced an audience at any theater. "They *are* young and I've heard that neither one of you has the least bit of control where Wes and Paige are concerned. So I guess it's for the best."

"What's that supposed to mean?" Troy demanded.

"Only that you take a toy every time you go see them and are spoiling them rotten. And I've heard that Dad can't bring himself to say no, so they get away with everything when they're with him."

Bobbie might have gotten away with her bald-faced lies if she hadn't dropped in a chair just then and begun filing her nails with far more deliberation than necessary. She was a study in concentration until Troy sailed a sofa pillow across the room and hit her in the head. Bobbie whipped it back at lightning speed, catching her brother totally off-guard.

Smiling with satisfaction, Bobbie growled in her gruffest voice, "Now, do my niece and nephew go with us or do I have to get rough with you?"

"They can come, they can come!" Troy cried in mock terror.

"You still have to ask Alice," Jake reminded Bobbie.

"I thought you might ask her. She's always been putty in your hands."

Jake smiled at the description. It was true. He had always been close to his oldest daughter, even though she was painfully shy. She was more open with him than she was with Maryanne or her siblings, and Jake had always nurtured their relationship. The only thing to ever come between them was Jake's decision for Christ. Alice had been very hurt when her father had explained how he had come to see his need for salvation.

"But what have you been up until now, Dad, if you haven't been a Christian?" Alice had asked.

"I've been someone who thought I could get to heaven

if I did my best and watched my step. I was leaving Jesus Christ completely out of the picture."

"So what you're saying is, if a person is good, it still won't be enough?"

"That's right, honey, the Bible says we get to heaven God's way, and that's through the death of His Son, Jesus Christ, who died to take away our sins."

"That's barbaric! I can't believe God would spurn our efforts just because we didn't choose to believe something so awful as Christ's death on the cross! I've read the Bible's account of the crucifixion, and, Dad, you can't tell me that God would honor such a horrendous act against His own Son!"

Jake had gone on to explain the best he could but Alice would have none of it. They had parted on good terms, but Jake's heart had been heavy. He found himself wishing they had attended Pastor Keller's church years before, when Alice had been younger and possibly more receptive to the gospel.

Today father and daughter were as close as ever, but Jake knew he had to tread lightly when the conversation turned to church attendance and salvation. Alice had made it quite clear that she thought her parents attended a church full of snobs who had the ridiculous notion that they knew the only way to heaven.

And as always, when Jake visited Stuart and Alice, their beliefs and the church they attended weighed on his heart. But he knew he did a good job of hiding this fact, since she and her husband always welcomed him with open arms.

"What brings you out on this cold January night?" Alice asked her father when he had settled himself on the sofa.

"Your sister. We're going camping this weekend, and Bobbie wants Paige and Wes to go with us." Jake would never have spoken so plainly if the children had been present, but he knew it was at least an hour past their bedtime.

Stuart and Alice looked at each other for a long time. They, like Jake and Troy, had never considered the idea. Suddenly Alice chuckled.

"Leave it to Bobbie to come up with something like that."

"She's pretty pleased with herself. She sent me because she was sure I could convince you."

Alice chuckled again. "Well, this time she's going to be disappointed. Paige has a drippy nose and I think it's too cold for them to go camping."

"Bobbie planned on them sleeping with her."

"We could plan on the next time you go," Stuart interjected. "Maybe it will be warmer."

Stuart Townsend was every inch the bank employee with his dapper suits and neatly trimmed beard and mustache. He never interfered with his wife's raising of the children, so Jake was aware that Stuart's comment about the cold was a very real worry.

"That's probably a good idea. I'm sure Bobbie will feel let down, but like you said, there's always next time." Jake didn't stay much longer, but before leaving, Alice led him into the twins' rooms so he could see them. The light from the lantern didn't disturb them in the least, and as always, Jake's heart swelled with love at the sight of his grandchildren.

Just as Jake expected, his younger daughter and son were disappointed about the twins not going with them. Jake pointed out that it was cold and maybe it would work out for the next time.

As it was, it rained very hard at the time Jake, Troy, and Bobbie were going to leave for their trip, and it continued to rain all weekend. Maryanne, who had planned to sew all weekend, laid aside her plans and the four of them played games and talked for hours. It was a wonderful homecoming for Bobbie. The only dark spot on the weekend was how late they all stayed up on Saturday night, causing them to oversleep Sunday morning and miss church. Bobbie had been looking forward to seeing everyone, but consoled herself with the fact that she started her new job the next day.

She took herself to bed when it was still early on Sunday, and with the lantern turned high she lay in bed and wrote in her journal.

January Seven, 1872

It's lovely to be home. The clock did not stand still as I hoped it would, and nearly everything and everyone changed. My parents look older, but they are in some ways ageless. I'm going to contribute to the household whether my parents like it or not. Oh Troy, you're so much fun. And Paige and Wes—thank You, Lord!

Tomorrow is the big day. I'll see Jeff. I hope he likes me. Mr. Taylor too. I've got to get to sleep. Good night, journal, I'll write again in a few days.

Bobbie turned the lantern down then and fell asleep while praying for a calm heart to face her new job in the morning.

nine

Bobbie wore a green dress for her first day of work. She spent a little extra time on her hair and was pleased with the way it curled softly around her face. Her fingernails, always long, were clean and well-shaped.

Maryanne had the day off, so Bobbie's send-off breakfast was a morning feast of omelettes stuffed with bacon and cheese, plus fresh muffins with jam, cider, and hot, strong coffee.

Bobbie left the house right after breakfast. Her coat kept her warm as she walked briskly away from home. She felt a little like a child on the first day of school as her lunch tin swung in her hand with every step. The shipping office was a welcome sight and Bobbie walked in the front door with a smile on her face.

May Taylor immediately rose from the desk in the corner and came toward her.

"Hello, Bobbie. It's good to see you." The two women embraced, and when May stepped away, Bobbie saw that there were tears in her eyes. "Don't mind me, honey. It's just that you're an answer to prayer and it's so wonderful to have you here."

"It's good to be here, Mrs. Taylor." Bobbie didn't say more and May could see she was close to tears herself. The two women had begun to talk about the workings of the office when Bill Taylor came in holding the hand of a young girl.

"Hello, Bobbie." Bill greeted his new employee warmly and shook her hand. They talked about her trip and whether or not she was settled in, and then May pulled the youngster closer to their circle of conversation.

"Bobbie, I'd like you to meet Marcail Donovan. Marcail, this is Bobbie Bradford. She's going to be working here at the office for awhile. Marcail's sister Kaitlin is married to our Rigg."

"It's nice to meet you, Marcail." Bobbie smiled kindly and held out her hand. Marcail must have instantly liked what she saw because she shook Bobbie's hand with enthusiasm.

"My sister's going to have a baby," Marcail informed Bobbie seriously.

"And you'll be Aunt Marcail," Bobbie replied with a smile. "I think that's wonderful. I have a niece and a nephew and they're so much fun. I know you'll love being an aunt." The little girl beamed at her newfound friend before May claimed Bobbie once again and began showing her the desk where she would do the majority of her work.

The shipping company was located in a spacious building on a corner lot. The office had a sectioned-off corner for a private office for Bill, whose window overlooked the side street. Bobbie's desk, formerly May's, sat in the opposite corner with a complete view of the entire room as well as the large windows that looked out over the loading area and the street.

May sensed immediately that Bobbie had a complete knowledge of the job. She knew everyone had his own way of doing things and wanted to leave Bobbie to her task as soon as possible. Ten minutes later May left so Marcail would not be late for school, telling Bobbie if she needed anything to knock on Bill's door.

May was not gone ten seconds when a woman came in wanting to send a package to San Francisco. Upon meeting Bobbie, the woman wanted complete details as to the whereabouts of May. Bobbie, with her kind attitude and ready smile, explained to her who she was and why May was not there. At the desk Bobbie recorded all the information for the package before accompanying the woman out to her buggy, where she gave Bobbie the large parcel she wanted sent.

The package wasn't so much heavy as it was awkward, and Bobbie walked back inside, peeking over the top of it as she moved. After closing the door she turned without looking and ran into someone whose arms came out and lifted the burden from her. Bobbie's head tipped back to see who was before her. Jeff Taylor stood regarding her with serious, almost hesitant eyes.

Bobbie grinned into those eyes, her own filled with friendship and something that might have been defined as tenderness. She had already given much thought as to how hard this might be for him.

"Hello, Jeff," she said softly. Jeff's relief was so great he sighed audibly.

"Hello, Bobbie." He smiled, his whole body losing its former tenseness. "I see Mom didn't waste any time in putting you to work."

Bobbie, trying not to laugh at the sigh and look of relief that had come over her co-worker's face, continued to grin at him.

"I don't mind. It's pretty routine and I have a tendency to get antsy if I don't have something to do."

They smiled at each other again, and Jeff mentally shook his head over the way he had tortured himself all through the night and that morning over how uncomfortable it was going to be working with Bobbie.

He had deliberately come into the office late, putting off what he was sure would be awkward: to find Bobbie handling a customer like a pro. He had watched her, unnoticed, from the doorway of the storeroom. Jeff was fascinated. Cheerful and efficient, she was not at all as he expected.

The only problem he could see was her obvious tendency to overdo. His mother would never have lifted a package as heavy as the one Bobbie had. May would have called to one of the men in the family for assistance. Jeff placed the package against the wall, taking note as he did that it was already wrapped for travel, and turned back to Santa Rosa's newest shipping clerk.

"Bobbie, in the future be sure to call one of us to help you with packages that heavy."

Bobbie was surprised. What was she there for if not to work? There was absolutely no way she was going to go running for help every time a large package came in. Why, the very thought of it!

Jeff was still staring at her, so Bobbie decided to reassure him. "I wouldn't lift something that I couldn't handle, Jeff."

Jeff smiled and kept still, having accurately read what was going on in her mind. He would let his father handle this one. They were discussing more aspects of the job, such as the storage room at the back of the building, the stage depot next door, and the hours both offices were open, when Gilbert came in.

"Hello, Bobbie." Bobbie could only stare at him.

"Gilbert?" She finally managed to say.

"It's me." Gilbert stated the obvious and waited for Bobbie to look her fill. He had been a boy when she left, only 13. Five years later he towered over her and was almost as filled-out as Jeff. Both men sported lean frames and broad shoulders. Their arms were corded with muscles, brought on by the daily tasks of lifting, loading, and packing every conceivable size of crate and package.

"Well, I see you're following in the same homely footsteps as your brother," Bobbie said, her voice becoming dry and giving the men a first glimpse of what working with Roberta Bradford would be like. "I suppose girls go out with you because they feel sorry for such an ugly little pup. Well, look at that smile I'm getting! And after all those insults! You're obviously very disagreeable too."

It was too much for the Taylor men; they couldn't hold their laughter. Bobbie joined them, and then a man came in with an armload of small boxes. Bobbie turned serious in the blink of an eye and the customer was explaining his need and paying his money in record time.

Gilbert was impressed with his first look at Bobbie in action. Gil wondered if his parents knew what a treasure they had found.

"Where's May?" Bill asked as he came out of his office and approached the desk where Bobbie was seated.

"She and Marcail left a little while ago."

"I'm sorry, Bobbie," Bill stated sincerely. "I had no idea you were out here trying to deal with the customers on your own." Bill stopped when his sons began to laugh. Bobbie didn't hear the explanation they gave their father because someone else had come in off the street and Bobbie moved to help them.

It was Bill's turn to watch his new employee in action, and he felt like May did—that he could cry over how good it was to have her with them.

The next hour flew by in a frenzy of activity, and no one was given any more time for socializing. At one point Jeff and Gilbert watched their father take a large box from Bobbie and tell her she was not to be lifting anything that heavy. Bill turned away as though the matter was settled, but both of the younger men could see that Bobbie had a mind of her own on this subject. It wasn't until after lunch that the situation came to a head.

"Bobbie," Bill said as he plucked, yet again, another heavy package from his newest employee's arms. "Am I or am I not your boss?"

"You're my boss," Bobbie admitted quietly.

"And as your boss, I've told you that you're not to be lifting articles that are too heavy."

"I'm not lifting too much," Bobbie stated in respectful logic.

"I think you are."

"Mr. Taylor, did you write and tell me you needed a shipping clerk, or did I misunderstand your letter?"

"Yes, I need a shipping clerk, but—"

"Then I'm only trying to do my job," the small blonde cut him off, her voice and posture a picture of respect. "I'm young, strong, and healthy, and I haven't lifted a thing today that was too much for me."

Bill could only stare at her. He had *never* had an employee stand up to him before. He was a reasonable man but his word was law. He only had to say something once to have it obeyed. And now this young woman with the beautiful green eyes and the adorable glasses perched on her nose, a woman who had to tip her head back to look up at him, was telling him she could lift and tote like his sons.

Bobbie waited a moment for her employer to say something, but when he remained silent and when someone else needed her, she went off without a word, thinking as she did that he had seen her point and the matter was settled.

Bill stood still and watched Bobbie handle one of his toughest customers. He stared in amazement when she actually wrung a smile from the old coot. A moment later he motioned Gil and Jeff, both of whom had again witnessed the entire conversation, into his office.

"Does she ever stop moving?" Bill came right to the point and his sons smiled.

"I think she took about five minutes to eat her lunch," Gil told his dad.

Bill nodded and was silent a moment. "I want you to keep an eye on her. Now, I don't mean for you to babysit her and ignore your own work, but if you see her lifting something she shouldn't, take it from her. If that's too distracting for you, then I'll talk with her again."

"Lay down the law, Dad, like you did today." There was a teasing glint in Jeff's eyes and Bill smiled.

'She's certainly a surprise,' Bill thought to himself, staying at his desk long after his sons exited. Bobbie wasn't a person that drew any attention to herself. If something needed doing, she did it in silent efficiency. Bill thought that might take a little getting used to.

He knew he had babied May over the years. When it came to some of the tougher jobs or customers, he had always dealt with them. When it came right down to it, May could have handled everything as easily as he did.

What he was feeling today might have stemmed from the fact that he kept forgetting Bobbie was there. She was so quiet and efficient that he was already taking her for granted. By enlisting the help of his sons, he hoped they would all be more aware of her.

The sight of Bobbie, looking at him through those glasses, confident and unwavering, came to mind. It would do them all a little good to have someone like her working around the office, and he would do whatever he had to do to keep her working there—that is, until she completed her plans for marriage. Bill found himself thinking that the guy who snagged Bobbie Bradford was one lucky fellow.

ten

"Are you going to work here all the time?" The question came from Marcail who was standing beside Bobbie's desk in the shipping office. It was near closing time and Bobbie was filling out some papers and preparing to leave for the evening.

"Well," Bobbie said slowly, "for awhile."

"I'm not going to work here when I grow up. I'm going to teach school like Katie."

"Katie is your sister?"

The little girl nodded. "Her real name is Kaitlin. She used to be Kaitlin Donovan but now she's Kaitlin Riggs because she married Rigg."

"And she's a schoolteacher?"

"Right. She's my teacher and Sean's too. He's my brother. He's 14."

Listening to all of this in thoughtful silence, Bobbie did not want Marcail to know that none of this was news to her. She had of course known Marshall Riggs, or at least *of* him, for years. And when he had married the schoolteacher, her mother had written and told her all about it.

Marcail was at Bobbie's desk because Rigg was in the office with his father. They had come in a few minutes ago, and Marcail, who had already decided that Bobbie was very nice, had come straight to her desk to talk.

"How was school today?" Bobbie asked her young companion, who was regarding Bobbie's long fingernails with dark, serious eyes.

"It was fine. Katie's pretty tired. She says it's because of the baby. Have you ever had a baby?"

"No," Bobbie answered softly.

"But you're an aunt?"

"Yes. My sister has five-year-old twins named Paige and Wesley."

"Twins!" Marcail's eyes grew very round. "Do you think Katie will have twins?"

A deep chuckle sounded behind them and both ladies turned to see Rigg listening.

"I'm not sure you should say that to your sister, Marc. She's so tired right now she can't think straight. Hello, Bobbie," Rigg continued. "You've grown up a little bit since I last saw you."

Bobbie smiled, almost mischievously. "You look the same, Rigg. A bit happier, perhaps, which I suspect has something to do with your recent marriage. Allow me to offer my congratulations on your having acquired a wonderful sister-in-law." Bobbie winked at Marcail on these words.

"Thank you," Rigg said as his own eyes began to sparkle. His father had said it was going to be fun having Bobbie around and he could already see why.

"Oh, I guess I should also offer my best wishes, since you now have a wife, and a baby on the way." Bobbie said this as though it had just come to mind.

Rigg, caught up in the spirit of Bobbie's teasing, bowed to her most formally and asked how the job was going.

"Very well, thank you. Most of it is routine, but the code system your father uses, along with all the different faces and names of the customers, is going to take awhile for me to learn."

"Something tells me you'll catch on with no trouble at all. We better go, Marc, so we can help with supper."

"'Bye, Bobbie. Maybe I'll see you tomorrow."

"I'll look forward to it," Bobbie told Marcail as she walked them to the door.

The clock on the wall told her it was past closing time, so Bobbie put the sign out and shut the front door. With the sun sinking rapidly it was growing chilly outside. Bobbie thought she best get home before it grew much darker.

"Mr. Taylor," Bobbie called softly through his office door, "I'm going to go now. I'll see you in the morning."

The door opened before she could walk away and Bill stepped out. "Thanks, Bobbie, for all your work."

"It was my pleasure. Do you want me at the same time tomorrow?"

"Yes. I think you should plan on working the same hours as you did today, except for Saturdays. Some of those you'll have off and on others you'll work until noon. And of course we're closed on Sunday."

Bobbie looked a little surprised to learn she would have some Saturdays off. Bill figured she was used to working an office where there was little or no help at all and having to put in ten-hour days for at least six and possibly seven days a week.

"All right, Mr. Taylor. I'll see you in the morning. Good night."

"Good night, Bobbie."

Bobbie's step was light as she walked the distance home. It had been a long day, but she was pleased with her work and believed her employer to be also. Still praying and thanking God for the way He provides and cares, Bobbie walked up the steps of her house.

❑❑❑

Rigg and Marcail headed right home as planned and entered the warmth of the house through the back door. This put them in the kitchen, where they hung their coats on hooks and then moved to help Kaitlin with supper.

Sean, who lived with his sister and brother-in-law, just as Marcail did, was nowhere to be seen. Marcail assumed his job and set the table. Kaitlin was stirring over a large pot and Rigg slipped his arms around her for a brief moment.

"Let me do this."

Kate surrendered the spoon easily. "Thanks, Rigg. Did you guys see Sean?"

"Isn't he here?" Rigg's face darkened with concern and some suspicion.

"No. I think he said he had to work today."

Rigg's face clouded with very real anger and his wife put her hand on his arm.

"He wasn't scheduled to work today and he didn't even come in to check. How did he think to get away with such a lie, Kate?" Rigg's voice had turned from anger to anguish over this betrayal. "He knew I would be at the store and he would be found out."

"I don't know, Rigg. There's just no figuring him out these days." Kate's voice was weary, and as always her father's face came to mind.

Sometimes it was hard to believe that just a year ago she had been living with her family in Hawaii. A wonderful, almost idyllic life. Her parents had been missionaries. Kate had lived there nearly all her life, and both Sean and Marcail had been born in Hawaii. Now things were so different.

Her parents had surprised her on her twentieth birthday by announcing they would be taking a furlough. They had sailed to California and stayed with her Aunt Maureen Kent, her father's older sister.

The trip had a wonderful beginning but it hadn't taken very long for things to turn for the worse. Almost upon arriving, her mother, Theresa Donovan, was diagnosed with tuberculosis. Mother's last weeks with them had been so brief, and then her father returned to the islands to settle affairs. That had been nearly a year ago. It seemed that every few months something arose to keep Patrick Sean Donovan II separated from his family.

At first the children stayed with their aunt in San Francisco, but that arrangement didn't work. They then headed north to Santa Rosa, where Kaitlin took a teaching position and met Marshall Riggs.

It was love at first sight for Marshall—"Rigg" to friends and family alike. But for Kate, whose world was a painful place with the loss of her mother and absence of her father, their relationship was strained.

But Rigg was not easily discouraged, and he lovingly befriended all three Donovans, eventually winning Kaitlin's heart. They had been married since October, and now Kate was due in August.

Kaitlin had kept in as close touch with her father as the mails would allow, but at times like this, when Sean was acting up, or on her wedding day, she missed his presence so much that she wanted to sit down and cry. It didn't help to be pregnant, teaching school, and in a constant state of fatigue.

"Sit down, Kate," Rigg instructed his wife, who had been standing next to him for a few minutes without saying a word.

"No, I'll get the biscuits ready."

"I've already done that." He led her to a chair and pushed a mug of coffee into her hand. For the first time Kate realized Marcail had set the table. The sisters looked at each other and Marcail smiled uncertainly.

She had never seen her big sister tired like this, and watching her brother grow daily more rebellious was really something new. It was hard to have Father gone, and the nine-year-old missed him a lot, but not like Sean did. In fact, to watch Sean, you'd think that Father was gone just like Mother and not coming back at all! Marcail took great comfort in the fact that he would return someday. If anything was bothering her right now, it was that Kaitlin was so tired and had to see a doctor because she was pregnant. Marcail didn't like doctors.

"Did you see Bobbie again?" Marcail, who had been working at not chattering when her sister was tired, simply nodded.

"You'll have to tell her sometime how much you liked her the very first time you met." Marcail nodded again. May had taken her to school and she had immediately told her sister all about Bobbie Bradford and how nice she had been.

"She wears glasses, Katie, and they make her awful cute. Do I need glasses?" Kate had told her no, even as she wondered about this woman who worked for her father-in-law. She knew that she and Jeff had been in school together and she knew the Bradfords from church, but beyond that Bobbie was a mystery.

Sensing that Marcail needed a hug, Kate reached for her. Marcail stood by her older sister's chair, secure in the embrace while Rigg continued to put supper on. They had just sat down to eat when Sean came in the back door.

eleven

The night was cold, but Jeff was in no hurry to get home. He had dropped Sylvia off at her sister's house and was taking the long way home. They had parted on good terms even though an hour ago she had been furious with him.

Conversation over supper was light and Jeff had been having a great time until Sylvia asked how work had gone that day.

"It went well. Bobbie is a hard worker and off to a great start."

"Bobbie?"

"Bobbie Bradford. She started work at the office today. I told you about it."

"No, Jeff, you didn't." Sylvia's voice had become very low and Jeff could see she was angry. It always amazed him at how quickly that could happen.

"I must have forgot. Well, anyway, she's doing great."

"I wasn't aware that your father was in the market for a new employee." She was still furious. Jeff, hoping she would calm down, answered carefully.

"He never advertised, but Mom needed a break, and when he found out that Bobbie was coming back into town and that she was experienced, he scooped her up."

"So you've known for some time that Bobbie was coming back to Santa Rosa?"

Jeff immediately saw his mistake and struggled to find words that would erase the anger from his date's face. "Sylvia, I'm sorry that I never mentioned Bobbie's return. But we don't talk about my job very often and it just never came up. I wasn't trying to hide anything from you."

Sylvia saw his sincerity, and knowing that she was overreaching, she tried to calm herself. She knew that her eyes weren't as pretty when she was angry and she never wanted Jeff to find her unattractive.

With her mass of blonde hair and startling blue eyes, most men did find her attractive. But Sylvia wasn't interested in what *most* men thought, just Jeff Taylor. Jeff of course didn't know that, since she did see other men and always let him know about it. But if she stayed with it long enough, she was sure she could bring him around, was sure she would see that spark of jealousy in his eyes that told her he cared. So far it hadn't happened, but Sylvia was patient. She had let him get away once before when they were just 17. It wasn't going to happen again.

An image of Bobbie and the way she looked at the lagoon picnic sprang to mind. 'You don't suppose she'd come back beautiful, do you?' Sylvia asked herself and then had to work at not laughing at the thought; it was simply impossible. Ladies did not laugh out loud at the supper table, and besides, she didn't want to explain to Jeff what she was thinking.

Jeff was blissfully ignorant of Sylvia's thoughts as they finished their meal and then parted company an hour or so later. Jeff was tired as he climbed the stairs to bed, but a light glowing faintly from beneath Gilbert's door propelled him to his brother's room.

"Gil," Jeff opened the door a crack, "are you up?"

"Yeah." Gil answered from the bed, where he had lain down with his Bible. He rolled to his side and propped his head on his hand as he watched Jeff drop into the room's only chair.

"Out with Sylvia?"

"Yeah, we had supper at the hotel. Their meat loaf is good." Then Jeff fell silent, staring at the floor.

"How did it go with you and Bobbie today?"

Jeff stared at his younger brother. Gilbert had always been able to read his mind, and sometimes it was very disconcerting. This time he had understood, without communication, that Jeff was nervous over Bobbie's return.

"I was fine as soon as I saw her and saw that *she* was okay. Before that I was sure it was going to be awful."

"She's pretty nice, I'd say, and no one would ever call her lazy." Both men smiled. Before the day was over they had both followed their father's orders and taken large boxes from her or just plain stopped her from lifting one. They were then able to witness a stubborn look cross her face, one that was so cute and determined it made them smile.

"Definitely not lazy." Jeff agreed and once again stared at the floor, causing Gil to wonder what was on his mind.

"What's wrong, Jeff? Did she say something that's bugging you?"

"Do you ever get the feeling that something is going to happen and you're not sure you want it to, but you can't do anything about it?"

"Not really. What do you mean?"

"I'm not sure myself, but I'm really afraid I'm going to hurt Bobbie all over again."

Gilbert was silent until his eyes dropped to the open pages of his Bible. "Can I tell you about what I was just reading, Jeff?"

"Sure." Jeff seemed almost relieved by the distraction.

"I'm in the book of Job right now, and I know you're familiar with the story, but I never read this without marveling at all he went through. He loses everything! And, Jeff, he didn't have a clue. I mean, he had no idea any of this was going to happen! In a very short time, however, his wealth is wiped out, all ten of his children die, and he ends up covered with boils.

"And then to make matters worse, his own wife is angry because he's still giving his allegiance to God, and this is what he says to her in chapter 2 verse 10: 'Thou speakest as one of the foolish women speaketh. What? Shall we receive good at the hand of God, and shall we not receive evil? In all this did not Job sin with his lips.'

"Do you see what I'm trying to say, Jeff? Job made a choice, a quick decision as to how he was going to react to those trials that are far more difficult than most of us will ever have to handle. He decided *not* to sin and here you are already telling yourself that you might hurt Bobbie.

"I think you should be saying just the opposite—that no matter what anyone else says or does, you, Jeff Taylor, are going to do the right thing by Roberta Bradford."

Staring at Gil, Jeff thought, not even his pastor was able to touch him as Gil just had. Of course it would help if he spent more time reading his Bible—Jeff was well aware of that.

"Thanks, Gilbert," Jeff answered solemnly before going to his own room. He didn't immediately fall asleep. In fact, he prayed for a long time about all his brother had said.

The next morning found Bobbie and Gilbert working together in the storeroom. Unclaimed packages were stacked on shelves against one wall. Bill's policy was to go through these shelves every other month and clear them for incoming packages.

At the same time, inventory was done and the supplies were checked and reordered for the month. Gilbert went from a position on his knees to a step stool, time and again, in order to reach all the shelves and check each box. Bobbie stood beside him making a list of the nearly depleted supplies as Gil called them to her.

At one point, when Gil was high on the stool, his elbow bumped a small box off the shelf. Bobbie never saw or heard a thing and chose that moment to look up and say something. Gil was off the stool in a shot, but the damage was done; Bobbie's glasses were broken.

"Bobbie, are you all right?" Gil was nearly frantic as Bobbie kept her head down, leading him to believe she was seriously hurt.

"Be careful where you step," Bobbie said softly, and it took him a moment to see that she was looking for her glasses. Gilbert found them at her feet and picked them up in two pieces.

"Bobbie, I'm sorry." He placed them in her hands and watched as she brought them nearly to her nose for examination.

"It's just that small hinge in the middle. I'm glad it's just the frames; my dad has a little tool to fix them. Unfortunately I'll have to go home to get it."

"Okay." Gilbert shot out the door to his dad's office. He didn't notice that other than Bobbie turning to watch him go, she stood absolutely still. A few minutes went by and Bobbie prayed that Gilbert would come back soon so she could explain she needed his help. It crossed her mind that since no one seemed to understand the extent of her eye problem, she might lose her job over this.

"Bobbie?" It was Gilbert's voice.

"Oh Gilbert, I'm glad—"

"No, it's Jeff."

Bobbie hesitated. For some reason she was reluctant to bother him.

"Jeff, do you know where Gilbert went?"

"Yeah, he's in talking with my dad."

"When he's through, could you tell him I need him?"

"Sure."

Bobbie heard the front door open and then Jeff walking away. She looked around her. Everything was very blurry. Well, not the shelf beside her, but that was because her shoulder was nearly touching it. Bobbie put her hand on the shelf for balance and then slid her foot carefully along the floor. She was afraid to actually take a step because she had no depth perception and everything looked so fuzzy and distorted.

Picking her way along slowly, Bobbie knew she was running out of shelf. She was also completely unaware of the fact that Gilbert and Bill were standing in the doorway watching her. Bill was silent and thoughtful as he watched his son approach Bobbie.

"Did you need me, Bobbie?" Gilbert asked from about two feet in front of her.

"Is that you, Gilbert?"

"It's me."

"Oh, good. I'm sorry I didn't explain—"

"You need to go home?"

"Right. But I need—"

"I'll take you right now."

Bobbie's features washed relief; he understood. He had also come close enough for her to see him. After watching her search his face with anxious eyes, he finally understood that he needed to draw nearer.

"Thank you." Bobbie smiled into his face, now so near her own, thinking he was the nicest guy on earth. "If you'll take me first to your dad's office, I'll explain."

"It's all right. He knows all about it." Bobbie need not know that Bill had learned much from his vantage point in the doorway.

Once out in the front office, Gil left Bobbie standing by the desk while he collected her coat. She heard conversation behind her but was again examining her glasses and paid no attention. When Bobbie's coat was dropped onto her shoulders she slipped into it and felt her arm taken as she was guided out the door. When they had gone about ten steps on the street Bobbie came to a halt.

"I need to tell you something, Gilbert. You need to be a step in front of me and let me take your arm. That way if you move I can feel it. If you come to a step, you'll need to say something or slow way down."

"I'll do just that, and by the way, I'm Jeff."

They had maneuvered into position, and Bobbie almost tripped when she heard who was escorting her.

"Where's Gilbert?" Bobbie asked in a small voice.

"He stayed at the office. I need to pick something up at Rigg's and I told him I would take you."

For some reason this was embarrassing to Bobbie. She felt that Gil was aware and concerned about her plight. Not that Jeff was being unkind, but she wasn't sure he really understood. She didn't really care to explain all over again about needing help, but in the next few minutes she wished she had swallowed her pride and explained.

"I take it you can find your way from here, Bobbie," Jeff said as he stopped before the mercantile. The shipping office was on a busier street than the mercantile and Jeff honestly believed Bobbie would have no trouble the rest of the way. He was gone before she could say a word. Bobbie found she was more frightened than she had ever been in her life.

Five minutes passed while she tried to calm herself. She did know exactly where she was, but had never been in this situation before. Maybe she could make it home.

Bobbie tried to think of where the boardwalk ended, if it was right at the corner of the mercantile or a little before. She held the broken spectacles up before her, thankful that the glass was intact. Moving slowly, Bobbie was able to get her hand on the side of the building. Afraid she would drop her glasses and never find them, they went into the pocket of her coat.

It was a chilly day and having to move slowly did nothing to warm her. Bobbie was almost to the steps when Rigg and Jeff noticed her from inside the store. They exited the building together and Bobbie was just about to step off into midair when Rigg's hand stopped her.

"Oh, thank you. Who's there?" Bobbie looked up at the blurry features.

"It's Rigg."

"Oh." Bobbie wanted to cry with relief. "I know you're terribly busy, Rigg, but I'm in a jam. I didn't explain to Jeff that I needed help getting all the way home, and now he's left. Troy is working at the livery, so maybe you could let him know I need help. I know you're busy." She finished in quiet embarrassment and Rigg led her to the bench in front of his store.

"Just sit here a minute, Bobbie. Jeff is still here."

Rigg wondered how long Jeff would have stood staring at Bobbie if he hadn't given him a shake. He seemed to be transfixed by the sight of Bobbie struggling along. Standing about ten feet away from her, he hurried forward after Rigg touched him.

"Here, Bobbie, let me help you."

Bobbie came to her feet and moved down the street with Jeff, wishing as she went that Gilbert had simply taken her home.

twelve

Bobbie was shivering uncontrollably by the time they reached the house. She stood just inside her front door and tried to calm down. Jeff had come a little farther into the living room and found himself staring at her once again.

In truth, Jeff was horrified over what he had just done. He asked himself how he could possibly have left her at the mercantile after witnessing the fact that she hadn't even recognized him in the storeroom, and again as they walked down the street she had thought he was Gilbert.

Something inside him had nearly torn in two as he had felt her arm trembling on his own on the walk home.

"I'm sorry, Bobbie. I feel ashamed I wasn't more sensitive to your needs."

"It's all right, Jeff. I should have explained. I need to talk with your father. It never occurred to me that your family didn't realize the problem I have with my vision." Bobbie's voice was soft, almost resigned.

"It's not going to change your status on the job, Bobbie. I can promise you that."

Bobbie only shrugged, clearly not believing him, and began to move across the room. That it was familiar to her was obvious, but Jeff was still pretty disturbed, and so he spoke up.

"Bobbie, if you'll just tell me what you need, I can get it."

"That's all right, Jeff. You don't need to stay. I'll come back as soon as I repair my glasses."

Jeff ignored her and deliberately moved to block her path. She stopped and stared up at him, noticing absently that she was feeling warmer.

Jeff brought his face down to what he believed to be very close. "Can you see me?"

"Pretty much."

Jeff moved again, this time until his nose was no more than an inch from hers.

"Now?"

"Yes."

"I want you to tell me what you need. I really can be of much more use than I was here in the last hour. So if you'll just tell me what you want, I'll get it."

Bobbie could see that he was determined. "I need to go into the kitchen."

Jeff turned his back to her. "Grab hold of the back of my coat." Bobbie grabbed on and was led into the kitchen.

"Now," she said, "over in the pantry there's a basket with odds and ends in it." She was quiet while Jeff retrieved it.

"What I need is a small tool that repairs the tiny hinges in these frames." Bobbie reached into her pocket for the glasses, and Jeff seated them both at the table.

Jeff nearly pressed the tool into her hand but instead picked up the glasses she had laid on the table. Bobbie didn't object, but leaned very close in an effort to see him work. He worked with careful precision, no easy task with Bobbie's nose almost touching his cheek. He noticed how nice her hair smelled and nearly told her so, but just then the back door opened and in walked Troy.

"Is that you, Dad?"

"What happened to your glasses?" Bobbie's question about who he was told him instantly, before he had even looked at her, that she couldn't see. Never was Troy more protective than when his sister couldn't see. Even as a child he could become almost violent if Bobbie were threatened when she was without her glasses.

"They broke at work."

"Are you all right?"

"Yes," Bobbie answered, but would have scowled at her brother had she seen the measured look he was giving Jeff. Although aware of Troy's scrutiny, Jeff felt it was best to ignore it.

"Got it!" Jeff said with great satisfaction. He meticulously wiped the fingerprints from the lenses before handing them back to Bobbie.

"Thanks, Jeff," Bobbie said with a relieved smile when she could see again. She then looked at her brother. "How come you're home?"

Troy shrugged. A family friend had come into the livery to say he thought he had seen Bobbie in front of the mercantile. Troy had been unable to concentrate after that so he took off to find out if it had been her. There had been no sign of her in the shipping office and Troy had nearly run home in a state of panic to find her. She had been out of their life for so long and it had scared him to think that something could happen to her when they had just gotten her back.

Troy never answered her, but for the moment Bobbie didn't seem to notice his quiet behavior.

"I need to get back to work."

"I'll go with you," Jeff said, and trailed silently after her. Troy's gaze had warmed slightly, and Jeff, not inclined to take things personally, figured Troy had been worried about his sister.

The walk back to the shipping office was equally as quiet as the exit from the house. Wasting no time once she was back inside, Bobbie went straight to Bill's office. She entered when he called "come in" and Jeff walked into the storage room to find Gil.

"I'm sorry, Mr. Taylor, I really am. It never occurred to me that you didn't know. I do have an extra pair of glasses that I'll bring in so I won't be completely out of commission if this happens again."

Bill listened in patient silence. She had apologized at least six times, and even though he had assured her that everything was fine, he could see that this had really shaken her up. She wasn't anywhere near this upset when she left, and Bill couldn't help but wonder what had happened while she had been gone with Jeff.

They continued to talk, and in time Bill could see that he was finally getting through to her, making her understand he wasn't at all upset and that she still had the job for as long as she needed.

But as they finished, Bill wondered if he should question Jeff. Maybe he could shed some light on why this very efficient young woman had been totally rattled over her glasses breaking.

"I should have explained to you," Gil said quietly.

"*I* should have seen with my own eyes that she needed help." Jeff was still reprimanding himself as he and Gilbert talked in the back room.

"Well, I'm glad you spotted her at the mercantile when you did and Rigg was able to grab her. Don't look so down, Jeff. You said you apologized."

"I know." But Jeff didn't look the least bit consoled. He left the storeroom to help two customers, and by the time Bobbie came out of Bill's office, he had formulated a plan.

"Bobbie," Jeff approached her immediately. "I was wondering if you'd let me take you to lunch today?"

"That's very nice of you, Jeff, but you don't have to do that." Bobbie was in no way fooled by this sudden invitation. Jeff was still feeling badly about the morning and Bobbie admitted to herself that it had been very upsetting, but it was nothing to feel guilty about for the remainder of the day.

"I know I don't have to. I want to."

Bobbie smiled at him, but didn't answer. He was different now than when she had known him before, very different. In fact, it was like getting to know a complete stranger. She knew his treatment of her that morning had not been out of rudeness and Bobbie wished she knew him well enough to know what was going on inside his head.

Jeff had no idea how handsome he looked to Bobbie at that moment, as he looked at her in silent entreaty. 'He really is wonderful to look at,' she told herself, still wishing she knew him better.

"I brought my lunch." Bobbie tried another tactic after a moment of silence.

"Then take it home with you." Jeff was not to be dissuaded.

Bobbie cocked her head to one side. "Has anyone ever called you pushy?"

"I think you just did," Jeff answered, and deliberately mimicked Bobbie's movement with his head.

Bobbie put her head to the other side and Jeff did the same. She told herself not to smile. After all, she reasoned, it would only encourage him.

"You're trying not to smile," Jeff said knowingly, and it was too much for Bobbie. Her grin nearly split her face.

"Will you go?"

"Yes."

Jeff's grin was triumphant and Bobbie shook her head in mock disapproval as she headed into the back room.

thirteen

The next hour saw a buzz of activity in the front of the shipping office. Gil and Bobbie worked steadily in the back, with an occasional trip out front to help Jeff and Bill.

The inventory would have been done long before lunch if Bobbie hadn't needed to leave. It was nearing 1:00 when Jeff looked up to see Sylvia walking in the door.

"I figured something like this must have happened. I can see you've been very busy, so I'll forgive you if you come to lunch right now, like you were *supposed* to an hour ago."

Jeff caught himself just before he began to babble. How in the world could he have forgotten that Sylvia asked him to lunch at her sister's? Now what was he going to do?

Sylvia, who had been smiling at him and was obviously in good humor, was beginning to frown over the way Jeff stood and stared at her in mute indecision.

"I'll be right with you," Jeff finally said, then rushed into the back room, leaving Sylvia alone.

"We're almost finished. Are you ready to leave?" Bobbie spoke as Jeff approached.

"Not exactly." Jeff said the words carefully, mentally measuring how he was going to explain.

"Is there a problem?" Bobbie asked with quiet sensitivity.

"Yes, there is, and it's all my fault. You see, Sylvia is out front. She asked me to lunch last night, and—"

"You forgot." Bobbie finished for him and raised her ordering sheet to her mouth. Her eyes told Jeff she was about to laugh, but Jeff didn't find the situation at all amusing. He had thought himself quite clever in coming up with this lunch idea to make up for the awful morning. Now this had to happen.

"Jeff." Sylvia's voice sounded from out in the main room and Jeff nearly groaned. Gilbert, who was listening from his place on the ladder, went out to give Jeff and Bobbie a little more time.

"Go with Sylvia, Jeff. She's waiting for you, and as I said, I have my lunch along."

"I'm sorry, Bobbie. You must think I'm very insensitive."

"Not insensitive, just forgetful," Bobbie said with another smile, and turned away so Jeff knew he could leave. His look had been heartbreaking, and Bobbie wished there was something more she could do to reassure him. He was going to have to get to know her, to understand she wasn't that sensitive.

Bobbie and Gilbert ended up eating their lunch together and talking like old friends.

"How go your wedding plans?" Gil asked kindly.

"Well, I'm not really rushing anything," Bobbie answered carefully, and Gilbert immediately keyed in on her hesitancy.

"I believe I was out of line just then and should apologize."

"Don't apologize, Gilbert. The truth is, Cleve has asked, but I haven't answered him. Marriage is a rather big step, and I'm still praying about it. Cleve told me to take all the time I need. He said he was sure he would eventually win me with his charm," Bobbie finished with a smile.

"I'm glad you told me, Bobbie. I'll be praying with you."

"Thanks, Gilbert."

The two fell silent. Gilbert searched for a change in the subject. "Will you miss living on the ocean?"

"You know, I really will," Bobbie admitted. "The sea is always so unpredictable and I love it."

"My sister-in-law Kaitlin grew up in the middle of the Pacific and she talks the same way. I've never even seen the ocean."

"You might have a chance someday. It helps to have relatives living right on the coast, but you never know, maybe when you get married you and your wife will honeymoon at the ocean."

"Are you applying for the job?" Gilbert teased her with a tender light in his eyes and then laughed without repentance when she blushed.

Jeff walked in on this scene. He looked from Bobbie to his brother for a moment, biting his tongue to keep from asking what Gilbert had said to make Bobbie blush.

Lunch had been miserable for Jeff. Sylvia was angry for most of the meal over the way he had gone into the back room and left her alone. Jeff had been preoccupied by the way Bobbie had turned away from him before he left. He thought she had been hiding her true feelings from him, masking how upset she was, and now he came back to find her laughing with his brother and then blushing like there was something personal between them.

"How was lunch?" Gil asked.

"Are you guys done in the back?" Jeff evaded the question.

"I'm going to finish up on my own," Gil told him. "Bobbie is free to help you out here."

Jeff nodded, carefully keeping his emotions off his face. He would have been surprised to know that both Bobbie and Gil knew something was bothering him. They just didn't know what.

❑❑❑

"I'm going to head home now, Jeff. Would you mind telling your dad?"

"I'll tell him. Maybe I should walk you home. It's getting pretty dark."

"Oh, I'll be all right, but thanks for the offer."

Jeff stepped forward when Bobbie lifted her coat from its peg on the wall. His touch was careful as he assisted Bobbie with her coat. Bobbie turned while she was buttoning to thank him. She looked up and opened her mouth to express her appreciation, but something in his face stopped her.

"You haven't had a very good afternoon, Jeff," she said instead. "Is anything bothering you?"

Jeff's heart would have been made of stone had he not responded to the tenderheartedness he saw in her eyes.

"Are you sure you're not upset about today?" Jeff finally asked the question that hadn't been off his mind for a moment.

"I was scared in front of the mercantile, Jeff, very scared, but I was over it before we ever left my house. And if you're still bothered about lunch, well, let's just say, I wish there was some way for you to know how well I understand. Everyone forgets things. And while we're on the subject of the way I'm feeling, can I say something?"

"Please do."

"I have feelings, Jeff. If you cut me I'll bleed, and if someone says something cruel to me I might cry, but I'm *not* made of crystal."

"I never said you were."

"But that's the way you're treating me. You can joke with me, Jeff, just like your father and Gilbert do, and you can even bump into me without apologizing for ten minutes. I'm not going to go to pieces like I did five years ago and run away, if that's what you're thinking. You push me and I just might push back."

Bobbie's chin had raised on these last words as did Jeff's eyebrows. 'She's right,' he said to himself. 'I've been treating her like she's a fragile piece of china, when plainly she's not.'

"All right, Bobbie Bradford," Jeff said with an air of determination. "I'll treat you with the respect you deserve and no more patronizing, *if* you'll always talk to me as bluntly and as honestly as you did just now."

Bobbie's hand came out and Jeff shook it. "It's a deal, Jeffrey Taylor, and by the way, you need a haircut."

The grin Bobbie gave Jeff on these words was nothing short of cheeky. Jeff would have smiled back and said goodnight before she sailed out the door, but he was too surprised to do anything.

"Like my dad said, she's not what we expected." He

addressed the words to the quiet office and then found himself whistling as he retrieved his own coat to head home.

fourteen

Jeff had supper at home, but left as soon as the meal was over to go to Rigg and Kaitlin's.

"What brings you out tonight, Jeff?" Kate wanted to know.

"Your haircutting skills, if you're up to it."

"She's not," Rigg said in a firm voice, but Kate ignored him. Kaitlin had been after Rigg for a week to let her cut his hair, but he always put her off. His worry over her fatigue was beginning to show, but even though Kate was tired, she wasn't an invalid.

"I'd be glad to cut your hair, Jeff. Why don't we go into the kitchen?"

"Kaitlin," Rigg pleaded softly, his voice laced with anxiety. Kate lingered next to him on the couch a moment and spoke with her face close to his.

"I'm fine, Rigg. You and Marcail did all the work for supper, so it's certainly not going to tax my strength to cut hair. I only wish Sean were here. He looks so disheveled these days."

Husband and wife exchanged a glance. Sean had been unpredictable lately, and the strain of it was worse than anything Kate had ever experienced. He did a tremendous amount of agreeing when he was face-to-face with you, but the minute your back was turned he did as he pleased. So far the things he did were not extremely serious, but there was a pattern of rebellion developing.

Rigg had already punished him for lying and also for disappearing after school with some friends and not coming in until almost bedtime. While the whole family prayed fervently for wisdom in dealing with Sean, most of the time Kate prayed for patience.

Kate and Jeff spoke easily while she clipped his hair. While not mentioning anything to Jeff, Kaitlin wondered if he knew how many times he referred to Bobbie.

"Bobbie said I need a haircut."

"Bobbie broke her glasses and I fixed them."

"That Bobbie sure is a hard worker."

"I made an agreement with Bobbie."

Rigg, who was reading the newspaper at the kitchen table, exchanged more than one glance with Kate over the top of Jeff's head. Everyone in the family assumed that Jeff and Sylvia were serious about each other. No one had ever taken the time to *ask* Jeff; it was just something they took for granted.

Jeff hadn't done much dating in the recent years, and it was nice to see him doing things and going places with Sylvia. It might also take a little adjustment if in fact they really weren't serious.

Jeff took his leave right after Kate finished with his hair, and Kaitlin and Rigg were then able to talk. They didn't come to any solid conclusions about Jeff, but they did understand that the Lord wanted them to pray about him, Sylvia, and Bobbie.

❑❑❑

Bobbie sat down that night and wrote to her aunt and uncle. She told them all about her first days of work and how it was to settle into home again. Troy was having supper at Carla's that night and her parents had retired early. She wrote about what happened with her glasses that morning, and then realizing just how tired she was, went to bed herself. Bobbie fell asleep so swiftly she didn't have time to talk over the day with her heavenly Father.

❑❑❑

"Thank you, Mrs. Gordon. I'm sure your package will go out this week."

Bobbie shut the office door as the woman strode swiftly down the street. Another day at the shipping office was complete and Bobbie was amazed at how swiftly time flew. It had been a great day, though. Jeff had scored a major victory by walking in with his new haircut. Bobbie had been surprised speechless, just as he had hoped. But Bobbie was rarely at a loss for words, and before it was over she had the Taylor men laughing the workday away.

No one was around when Bobbie was ready to leave, so she let herself out and shut the door. Her walk home was uneventful—in fact, it was very quiet. Entering the house, Bobbie was intent upon asking her mother what was going on in town. She found her in the kitchen throwing provisions in a large basket.

"Oh Bobbie, I thought I was going to have to leave a note. Your dad and Troy have already left for the Mickle-sons'. Their barn is on fire and the wind is blowing it toward the house. Gather some quilts and get them to the wagon. Your dad hitched the horse for us and I'm almost ready to leave." All of this was said with an air of urgency, but no panic.

Bobbie reacted in kind, racing to do as she was bid but with no hysteria or confusion. Within five minutes the Bradford women were on their way. Maryanne handled the horse and wagon efficiently and they arrived on the scene minutes later, joining Mrs. Mickleson and a few other ladies from the church. May Taylor was among them.

The women embraced and then talked. "Mic always lights a lamp in the barn but he's always so careful. I can't think how this could have happened."

Information on how the fire started was going to have to wait. Right now all the men were occupied with putting the flames out, or at the very least directing them from the tall farmhouse that loomed in the sky some 50 feet away.

The women who had come on the scene offered their help in one form or another. May offered to take the Mickleson children back to her house for supper and to spend the night. Lu Mickleson accepted gratefully and Bobbie offered to help round them up.

Mrs. Mickleson pointed out ten-year-old Brian standing at the corner of the house and Bobbie headed in that direction, only to have him move before she got there.

The heat from the barn hit Bobbie full in the face as she rounded the house and her eyes squinted against flames. She prayed for safety for her family and the others working. Brian had moved close to the fire and Bobbie called to him, hesitant to go further. Her shouts went unheeded and she knew she was going to have to go and get him.

She was only a few feet away from catching him by the back of the shirt when he darted away from her to circle the burning barn. Determined now, Bobbie followed without thought.

She hadn't gone ten steps when a pair of strong arms literally lifted her off the ground and bore her toward the house. Jeff began to shout the moment he put her on her feet.

"What in the world do you think you're doing?"

"I have to get Brian. Your mother is taking him and all the kids to your house." Bobbie's voice was equally as loud.

"Stay here!" Jeff commanded and ran toward the flames. He was back in less than a minute holding Brian's arm and walking so fast that the ten-year-old had to run to stay on his feet.

"Brian," Bobbie said sharply in her anxiety, "your mother wants you! Go to her immediately!" The boy left without a word and Jeff waited only a moment before once again letting Bobbie see his anger.

"That was incredibly stupid!"

"It was not stupid. I had to get that boy and I noticed *you* didn't hesitate to run right toward the flames!"

"That's different!"

"It is not!"

"Yes, it is. You're just too mule-headed to see it."

"How dare you call me a mule—" Bobbie's furious tirade was cut short by a flash of lightning, an unusual occurrence in Santa Rosa. The crowd in the yard and around the Mickleson barn only had time to look up before the deluge began.

Cheers of "hallelujah" and "praise the Lord" were heard from every corner. Their anger forgotten, Jeff and Bobbie looked at each other and laughed. Jeff scooped the small blonde into his arms once again and swung her around. They were still laughing when he set her on her feet.

"Bobbie," Maryanne called as she approached, "are you all right?"

"We're fine. Where are Dad and Troy?"

"They came over when it started to rain and I started to worry when you didn't come back."

Maryanne had a quilt in her arms and put it around her daughter.

The group stood, over 30 of them, a cold but grateful mass, until the flames were little more than smoking timbers. About half the barn would have to be rebuilt, but no animals were lost and no one had been hurt while fighting the fire.

Pastor had come on the scene to help and he led the group in a prayer of thanksgiving for God's protection and for the rain that minimized the loss and possibility of injury.

Maryanne took the food she had brought into the Mickleson home and then rejoined her family at the wagon. The rain had slackened. Both Bill and Jeff were there talking with Bobbie, who sat in the back with Troy.

"Jeff tells me you're chilled to the bone. You get right into bed when you get home."

"I always knew Jeff was a big tattletale." Bobbie tried to joke, but her shivers were nearly rattling her teeth out.

"I mean it, Bobbie. I don't want you coming down with something. If you feel a cold starting just stay in bed. If I don't see you by 8:00, I'll know you needed rest."

Bobbie was too cold to argue and Bill left before she could say anything. Jeff peered a bit anxiously into the back of the wagon.

"If you don't come in tomorrow I'll come by and see you."

"Thanks, Jeff."

"Good night," Jeff said to the family in the wagon and then watched as they disappeared into the dark.

fifteen

Bobbie felt great the next morning and was on the job at ten to eight. Bill questioned her closely until he was satisfied that she was really feeling well. Bobbie's smile was a bit indulgent as she answered his questions.

"All right, Bobbie," he said when he caught her look. "Just humor me. You're under my care now and I take my responsibility seriously."

"I know you do. That's why your sons keep taking packages from me that I'm perfectly capable of lifting."

Bill was surprised that she was aware of their watchful care, but was quick to recover. "Like I said, humor me."

They smiled at each other and then Bill told Bobbie that he would be uptown for most of the morning.

Gilbert didn't come in until close to 9:00. He arrived to find the shipping office packed with clients. Nearly 20 people sat on the benches and milled around the windows. The morning stages were late and these people were the overflow from the small stage office next door.

The stages arrived within minutes of each other and Jeff showed up to meet them. He and Gil helped unload and load both passengers and packages before heading back to the empty shipping office. Bobbie had taken a seat at the desk and was working on the never-ending stream of paperwork.

"I didn't think I was going to see you today." Jeff had taken one of the two chairs that sat opposite the desk.

"You sound like your dad," Bobbie commented as she laid her pencil down and removed her glasses. Jeff watched as she rubbed the little marks left by her spectacles on the bridge of her nose.

"Do they always leave those marks?" Jeff asked, leaning close now.

"Not always, but they do pinch some." Bobbie continued to rub her nose. When she replaced the glasses she found Jeff watching her with concern.

At some point in the last few days they had become friends. It felt wonderful, Bobbie thought, to know that Jeff was her friend. He cared about her and liked working with her, and she felt the same about him.

Bobbie smiled at Jeff's concerned look and his thoughts moved in the same direction as her own. What a good friend Bobbie was turning out to be. She was fun and kind, and he genuinely enjoyed being with her.

Jeff and Bobbie were still sitting and talking quietly with each other when the office door opened.

"Well, hello." Sylvia's voice came from just inside the door and both Jeff and Bobbie turned to greet her. Jeff, knowing her well, noticed instantly that she was upset about something.

"Sylvia, come in." Jeff smiled solicitously and offered his chair, but Sylvia's look was frosty. Jeff sighed. He wondered what he was in trouble for now. A mental rundown of the last few days told him he hadn't forgotten any more dates with her and it wasn't her birthday. He figured he'd have to wait and see. Sylvia never kept her anger to herself for very long, so he was certain to hear the cause before the day was out, and quite possibly within the hour.

"I can't stay. I just stopped in to say hello. It's good to see you, Bobbie."

"You too, Sylvia. How have you been?"

"Fine, and yourself?"

"Fine," Bobbie answered with a smile.

The question was sincere and so was Sylvia's, but that was only because seeing Bobbie was such a relief. She wasn't beautiful. In truth, she wasn't even pretty. Oh, her hair looked better and she was no longer straight-up-and-down, but the glasses were just the same and she wasn't a bit taller. She still had the soft aura of a child.

The thought made Sylvia relax. That must have been why Jeff was staring at her so intently when she came in. Jeff thought of Bobbie as a little sister.

"Well, I'm headed uptown so I can't stay." Some of Sylvia's irritation with Jeff returned when he didn't beg her to stay longer or offer to go with her.

"I'll walk you to your buggy."

"You don't have to," Sylvia assured him, but was pleased when he followed her.

"'Bye, Sylvia," Bobbie called, and the older woman gave her a smile and a wave. Bobbie sat back down in her desk chair.

"Wow!" Was the only word that would come to mind, and she said it out loud.

"What's wow?" Gil wanted to know as he came from his father's office where he had been working.

"Sylvia," Bobbie answered. "I thought she was pretty when we were kids, but now—" Bobbie let the thought hang, and Gilbert watched her as she stared off into space. She was still just sitting when Jeff returned.

"Did you think she wouldn't be as pretty?" Gil wanted to know.

"No, but I didn't think you could improve on Sylvia. I mean she was always the most beautiful girl in school, but now she looks like an actress you'd see on the stage. Her hair and eyes are more wonderful than ever."

Both men noticed that there was a tiny note of envy in Bobbie's voice and the thought saddened them. Sylvia was attractive and they were among her admirers. But both of them found Bobbie delightful, and the idea that she would wish herself to be anything other than she was made them both regretful.

Bobbie realized just then that the Taylor brothers were staring at her. "Have I said something wrong?" she asked cautiously.

"No, no," they rushed to assure her. Neither one had any idea how to tell Bobbie how they felt about her, so she was left in some confusion over their odd behavior.

Bill came back an hour or so after lunch. No one had taken any time to eat so he sent his sons and Bobbie out of the office.

"I don't want to see you back here for at least an hour." With these words he saw them out the door and shut it behind them.

"Well, I guess he told us," Bobbie laughed. "Now, I brought my lunch today, but, Jeff, you still owe me lunch out *and*, since you have such a poor memory, I think you should treat Gilbert too."

"Is that right?" Jeff's hands had come to his hips and he stood regarding the sassy little blonde beside him.

"Yes, that's right. Don't you agree, Gilbert?"

"I'll agree to anything for a free meal."

Jeff could see that he was outnumbered and gave in gracefully. Once at the hotel, they all ordered the special of the day and the men finished their meal with pie. Sipping her coffee as they made short work of dessert, Bobbie told herself to make time for the post office before she returned to work. The rule in the Bradford family was simple: Anyone who had time to get to the post office brought home the mail.

Bobbie told her lunch companions that she would see them back at the office, but when she told them where she was going, they decided to go with her. Bobbie had two letters from Jenner, one from a girlfriend and the other from Cleve.

They were back at the office before Jeff realized she had received mail from a man. He couldn't resist teasing her, even though he was well aware of her engagement. The letter was lying unopened on her desk, and when things were quiet, Jeff spotted it.

"What's this?" Jeff said with delight. "You're not getting mail from a man, are you, Bobbie?" Jeff had picked up the letter and was examining it closely. "What's his name now? Oh, Cleveland. Hmm, what do you suppose he has to say?"

"Does the word 'busybody' mean anything to you, Jeffrey? Now give that back to me." Laughing, Bobbie had come out of her chair. She reached for the letter but Jeff sidestepped her. He held it behind his back.

Bobbie stood with her arms folded across her chest, her foot tapping the floor. "Are you going to give me that letter?"

"Just like that? Give it back when I'm having such fun teasing you?" Jeff brought the letter out and waved it in the air like a trophy. Bobbie made a grab for it and felt her fingernail scrape against his hand.

"I've scratched you!" Bobbie was aghast. She had never done such a thing before.

"It's all right."

"No it isn't. I'm going to cut these nails right now."

"No," Jeff nearly shouted as Bobbie headed for her handbag. "I'm fine, Bobbie, don't cut your nails on my account."

"Jeff, I scratched you!" Bobbie repeated herself as if that explained everything.

"It's nothing. Look." Jeff thrust his hand out and Bobbie saw that he was right. It was a tiny mark on the surface of the skin that would probably disappear if he rubbed it.

"Please don't cut your nails."

"It could have been much worse, Jeff. I really shouldn't keep them so long. And really, Jeff, I can't believe it even matters to you."

"I just think your hands are very pretty and that it'd be a shame to cut your nails."

Bobbie was not sure why, but having Jeff tell her that her hands were pretty made her inordinately happy. It also made her blush. To hide her embarrassment Bobbie turned away and sat back at her desk. But Jeff had seen the flushing of her cheeks, and as he set the letter back on the desk and stopped his teasing, he understood with sudden and complete clarity why someone would ask Bobbie Bradford to marry him.

sixteen

The Micklesons' barn fire was the talk around town for the next few days and on into Sunday. Pastor Keller announced that weather allowing, there would be a "barn-building day" on the following Saturday.

The Micklesons were descended upon after the service with promises of attendance and help. Bobbie was thronged also. She couldn't believe how many people came up to hug her and welcome her home. It felt wonderful. When the people surrounding her finally cleared, Bobbie looked down to see Marcail at her side.

"Hi, Bobbie."

"Hi, Marcail. How are you?"

"I'm fine. I want you to come and meet my sister."

Marcail grabbed Bobbie's hand and was led to the Riggs' wagon. Kate was already seated.

"Katie, this is Bobbie. Bobbie, this is my sister Kate."

"Hello," Bobbie greeted Kaitlin with a smile, and Kate responded to the warm friendliness she saw there.

"It's nice to finally meet you, Bobbie. Marc has been planning this meeting for two days. I'm sure she told you I was expecting."

"Yes, she did. Congratulations."

"Thank you, but I'm afraid it's been a disappointment to Marcail that I haven't come to the shipping office to meet you. The truth is, I'm tired all the time and I just wasn't up to it. She finally figured out we would see each other here."

Nathan Taylor came on the scene just as Kate finished talking, and whatever reply Bobbie was going to make was cut short.

"Hi, Nate," Bobbie greeted him cheerfully. "I forgot to tell you yesterday that a girl came in looking for you. She said she'd see you Monday, and I think she said her name was Brenda." Bobbie had given this message softly so as not to embarrass Nate, but his face flamed nonetheless.

"Now there's no reason for you to be blushing like that, Nathan." Bobbie's voice was her most sarcastic. "I know for a fact that she only came in to see if you were just as homely on Saturday as you were when you left school Friday."

The teasing did the trick. Nate instantly relaxed, and Kate, who had been listening from the wagon, fell for Bobbie just as her sister had.

"Well," Nate decided to give as good as he got, "I might be homely, but at least I'm not short." Nate took great delight in his being four years younger than Bobbie and many inches taller.

"Is that right?" Bobbie cocked her head to one side in a way that was becoming familiar to them all.

"Yes, that's right."

"What you don't know, Nathan, is that I could be taller. I just don't want to be."

"Is that right?" Nate imitated her perfectly, and before

Bobbie could reply, the Riggs' wagon was converged upon by Bradfords and Taylors.

Everyone seemed to be talking at once, and after a few minutes May and Maryanne decided they should all have lunch together. A hasty potluck was planned and Maryanne and Jake headed home to collect their food. Marcail begged Bobbie to ride with them, so she found herself in the back with her new little friend and a very quiet Sean, whom she had just met.

The wagon was already moving when Jeff hopped aboard and made himself comfortable on the blankets. He tipped Sean's hat over his eyes, gave Marcail a quick hug, and smiled at Bobbie, but his thoughts seemed far away and the ride to the Taylors' was fairly quiet.

❑❑❑

"I thought Jeff was coming to lunch," Sylvia's sister commented when she came in alone after church.

"We had a fight."

"Again?"

"Yes, again," the younger girl snapped. "He's not doing anything right. He wanted me to have lunch at his house today."

"So why didn't you? Surely you didn't come here on our account." Sandra's voice was dripping with malice.

She had thought it was going to be such fun having her sister stay with her, but Sylvia hadn't grown up at all in the years she was away from Santa Rosa. She was as self-centered and conniving as she had been when they were kids. Carl had been on her to get Sylvia to end her visit and go home, but Sandra didn't know how to tell her, so she not only had to put up with Sylvia's childish behavior but her husband's angry words to boot.

"I didn't want to have lunch there," Sylvia went on as though explaining something to a simple child. "I can't ever get Jeff alone at his house. There are people everywhere. And I'm never going to get Jeff to propose to me if I don't get him alone."

Sylvia had told herself that she was never going to tell Sandra her plans for Jeff, but she was growing desperate. And just as she suspected, this news was not well received by her sister.

"Sylvia, you can't be serious."

"I don't know what you mean," Sylvia stated, but it was a lie.

"If you're in love with Jeff, why are you seeing other men?"

The younger woman tossed her head with an indignant sniff. "I should have known you wouldn't understand. Not all men are like Carl, you know. They don't all just fall at your feet the moment they lay eyes on you. Sometimes the woman has to work a little harder to get what she wants."

Sandra's look was piteous and it made Sylvia furious. Without a word she pounded up the stairs. The slamming of her bedroom door echoed throughout the house.

Carl, who sat quietly on the sofa being ignored, watched his wife. When she finally turned to face him, he felt guilty for the anguish he saw there. Some of it was his own fault. He hadn't realized just what Sandra had to deal with when it came to Sylvia, and he had put even more pressure on her.

His compassionate look was like a lifeline to his wife, and when he held his hand out to her, she joined him. Sandra cried against her husband's chest like she had never cried before. They talked for a long time and came to some painful decisions. They wouldn't try to change things overnight, but Sylvia was not going to go on staying with them forever—this much was clear. What wasn't clear was how she would be told, by whom, and when.

❑❑❑

Bobbie opted to sit at the "kids'" table. There wasn't enough room at the big kitchen table for everyone, so a smaller table was set up in the living room for the younger family members.

Troy and Gilbert were both younger than Bobbie, but she took a place in the living room with Sean, Marcail, and Nate. Laughter was plentiful around the small table, thanks to Bobbie. Even Sean was beginning to thaw. The small blonde had that effect on people.

"So how young were you when you learned to swim?" Bobbie was questioning the Donovan children about growing up in Hawaii.

Marcail shrugged. "We just always knew."

"Our mother always said we could swim before we could walk." This was the first time Sean had offered information without a direct question and Bobbie believed they were making progress.

"I tried swimming when I lived in Jenner," Bobbie told them with a laugh. "I thought I would die."

"You almost drowned?" Marcail asked with wide eyes.

"No, it was *freezing*. I didn't think water got that cold. Every inch of me was blue. I think I shivered for two days."

"The water was always warm in Hawaii."

"I would have loved that, Sean. Anyway, I didn't try it again for a long time, but eventually I did learn to swim in the ocean and I really enjoyed it."

The remainder of the conversation was relaxed and it wasn't long before everyone was finished eating. There were more than enough hands to help in the kitchen, so Bobbie followed Marcail outside to the swing. It was cold, but the girls bundled into their warm coats and hoped it wouldn't rain.

"I'm freezing, Marcail," Bobbie called to her after the nine-year-old had the swing high in the air. "Did you want to go in pretty soon?"

"Let's go to the barn. It'll be warmer in there."

Marcail worked the swing down to a gentle glide and jumped the few feet to the ground. She and Bobbie hurried toward the barn.

"Oh, this feels heavenly," Bobbie exclaimed as the warmth of the barn enveloped her.

"Let's go up to the loft."

"I really don't think I want to climb that ladder." Bobbie said the words apologetically and Marcail didn't press her. Instead the two flopped into a stall filled with fresh hay. Reclining like princesses, they talked like best friends. They had been in the barn for about 20 minutes when Marcail heard her name being called.

"That's Katie. I've got to see what she wants. Don't go away." Marcail was up and running in the next second, slipping quietly out the barn door that stood ajar.

Bobbie removed her glasses and rubbed her nose. She felt something poking her in the leg and stood to adjust her position. But a moment after she stood she felt her glasses slip from her cold fingers. Not wanting to step on them, Bobbie stood immobile, then knelt carefully and began to feel along the ground.

A well-known feeling of frustration rose within. To be so dependant on a pair of wire rims filled with glass was at times more frustrating than Bobbie felt she could endure. But whenever these thoughts came to mind, a Bible verse came with them.

It was 1 Corinthians 10:13, and Bobbie knew it by heart: "There hath no temptation taken you but such as is common to man; but God is faithful, who will not suffer you to be tempted above that ye are able, but will with the temptation also make a way to escape, that ye may be able to bear it."

The temptation, Bobbie knew at the moment, was the fact that she was about to blow her stack. Instead she prayed.

"I need Your help, Lord. I can't see, and that always scares me a little. Please send Marcail or someone out here to help me before I panic." Bobbie carefully sat back down in the hay. She felt around her coat and the hay surrounding her, but stayed where she was. She always caught the worst trouble when she moved.

The barn was feeling quite chilly when Bobbie finally heard someone enter.

"Who's there?"

"Where are your glasses?"

Bobbie sighed at the sound of her brother's voice. "Hi, Troy. They're in front of me somewhere. Be careful where you step."

"I'll light a lantern." It was Jeff's voice but Bobbie didn't greet him. This was the second time she'd had glasses trouble since she got back. Why did Jeff have to witness both episodes? Bobbie found it humiliating.

'That's just your pride, Bobbie, and you know it,' the stranded woman rebuked herself, and waited while the search began. They were of course in plain sight to anyone who could see, and it was only a minute before Jeff said he had found them.

"Are they broken?"

"I'm afraid so. It's the same place as before, though, and not the glass."

"Dad might have something with him, Bobbie. I'll take these to the house. Are you okay where you are?"

"Sure. Thanks, Troy."

Bobbie wasn't all right where she was. She was cold and feeling a little lost without her sight, but she didn't want Jeff to know that. After listening to footsteps exiting the barn, Bobbie brought her knees up and wrapped her arms around them. Her breath came out in a gasp when she heard feet on the floor very near her.

"I'm sorry, Bobbie," Jeff's voice was pained. "I thought you knew I was still here."

"That's okay," Bobbie's voice shook.

Jeff could see that it wasn't okay, but kept the thought to himself. He could only imagine how frightening it would be to be practically blind, albeit temporarily.

"I'll come and sit beside you so you'll know where I am." Bobbie sat very still when Jeff sat down, and neither one spoke for a moment.

"I thought we were friends."

"We are," Bobbie answered tentatively, wondering what direction the conversation would take.

"Then why are you embarrassed in front of me about losing your glasses?"

"I was hoping you wouldn't notice."

"I notice a lot of things. Now tell me why."

Bobbie spoke so softly that it was almost a whisper. "You feel unbelievably vulnerable when you can't see, Jeff. To have you come in and me not know it, then stay and not see you, just adds embarrassment to that vulnerability. I suppose it's pride, but it's hard to have you see me in this position."

"Thank you for telling me," Jeff said simply and put his arm around her. Bobbie laid her head against his shoulder and felt instantly better, but then realized she had a question of her own.

"Jeff, were you upset today when you got into the wagon?"

Jeff hesitated.

"Just tell me if I'm out of line."

"Sylvia and I had a fight, but I can't really discuss it with you."

"That's understandable. I'll be praying that you can clear the air soon."

"Thank you."

The conversation moved to other things and Bobbie was a good deal warmer by the time Troy returned. Bill had produced the needed tool to fix the glasses, and when Troy returned them, he said it was time to go. Everyone felt the afternoon was a wonderful success and most parted knowing they would see one another at the barn-building, if not before.

seventeen

Bill gave Jeff a choice about where he wanted to spend Saturday—at the Micklesons' or at the office. Jeff chose to work on the barn, and since it was Bobbie's full day off, both Nate and May were in to help Bill.

All the Bradfords were at the Micklesons' and the day promised to be clear. About 20 men were on the scene to help, and half that amount of women came around 11:00 to prepare lunch. Laughter and hard work were plentiful, and at the end of the day everyone was tired but feeling the rewards of a job well done. The Micklesons were thrilled with the work and sent everyone off with their repeated thanks.

When Bobbie retired for the night she reached for Cleve's letter. She had already written back to him but was having a hard time placing her feelings. She read the letter again and again in an attempt to know her own heart.

Dear Robbie,

How is work going? It's in my heart to say, 'I hope it's going well,' but you know I wouldn't mean it. Please come back. I know you said it would be October at the earliest but I still don't understand why. Your dowry doesn't matter to me. I've said this to you in person, but you don't believe me. I'm trying to be understanding about how long you've been away from your family, but my worry that you'll find someone else when you're there and never come back to Jenner and to me, is always on my mind.

I told myself not to mention any of this, but as you can see, that's all I've done. I was in to see Jasper yesterday. He looks well, but the office wasn't the same without you. Church feels just as lonely without you at my side. Please write to me.

I've got a surprise for you—I'm coming to Santa Rosa for a visit. I'll have to let you know the date and how long my stay will be. Maybe your boss would let you have a few days off.

Please write me as soon as you receive this.

Yours alone, Cleve

Still fully dressed, Bobbie sat on the edge of her bed for a long time. She wasn't even excited about Cleve coming to see her. Why was that? They were very close and she always enjoyed his company. In fact she always felt wonderful when they were together, and Bobbie knew why: Cleve thought she was beautiful.

Bobbie knew very well she wasn't, but that was the way every girl wanted her spouse to feel. And he wanted to marry her. Bobbie had only been on one date and that had been the ill-fated one with Jeff. She had never dated in Jenner; in fact, she and Cleve never dated. At first he came to the office to see her and then he would call around in the evenings at her aunt and uncle's home. He never tried to get her alone or make any advances toward her. Bobbie had been completely nonplussed when he had proposed one night three months ago, while Jasper and Joanne had been busy in the kitchen.

"What did you say to me?" Bobbie had asked.

"I said, Robbie, will you marry me?"

"Are you serious, Cleve?"

"Never more so."

"But we've never even talked about this."

"So let's talk now," Cleve said as he took her hand, touching her for the first time. Bobbie had been too stunned to speak. It was a wonderful thing to know that someone desired her for a wife, and it was simply lovely to have Cleve holding her hand so tenderly within his own, but it certainly wasn't as simple as he made it sound.

They had talked about little else in the weeks to follow, or rather Cleve had talked and Bobbie had listened. He had every imaginable argument as to why they should be married. The only thing he never mentioned was love. Bobbie said as much one night.

"I've never tried to analyze it before, Robbie, but I do know that I feel something for you that I've never felt for anyone before. I'm not at all worried that we're not gazing into each other's eyes like lovesick teenagers. Our marriage would be built on commitment and trust. And love, if not now, would come in time."

Cleve had kissed her then, the only time. Bobbie had been a little dazed after the kiss and even more so when he told her she was beautiful. She was also more confused than ever.

Bobbie's reverie was interrupted by a knock on her bedroom door.

"Come in."

"It's me, Bobbie."

"Hi, Mom."

"I saw the light under your door. Everything okay?"

"Not really, but I wouldn't know how to tell you what's wrong."

"Cleve?"

"Cleve." Bobbie answered, glad that her mother understood. "Do you know, Mom, that when he kissed me I thought I would melt? Does that make me kind of... promiscuous?"

"No," her mother said tenderly and felt tears sting her eyes.

"I also like it when he holds my hand."

"I'm sure you do. I would say that's pretty normal. Did Cleve kiss you often?"

"Just once."

"But wonderful kisses or not, you're not sure you want a lifetime of that?"

"Right. I mean, marriage is more than intimacy, isn't it? And I want to be sure that we can live as man and wife in every room of the house for the next 40 years. No regrets, do you know what I mean?"

"I know exactly what you mean," Maryanne answered calmly, but her heart was crying out to God. 'Oh please, Lord, give her a godly man who will cherish her as I've been cherished by Jake.'

"You better get some rest," Maryanne said after a moment of quiet.

"He's coming to visit."

"So you said. Now maybe that will settle the whole thing. He'll come and your father and I will loathe him on our first meeting and that will be the end of that."

Bobbie laughed. "I'm afraid it's not that easy. You'll probably think he's the greatest."

"Well, he does have one thing going for him—he's in love with my daughter." Maryanne stopped with her hand on the door. "Bobbie, what does that look mean?"

"Actually, I can't really say that we are in love."

"Do you mean that Cleve has never told you he loves you?"

"No, he hasn't. We've talked about it, and I'm not sure I love him either, but Cleve believes our marriage will be built on other things, and that love will come later."

Maryanne appeared pensive. *Alarmed* better described her mood, but she didn't want her daughter to know how dismayed she was.

"Bobbie, answer one question for me: Are you afraid that if you don't marry Cleve, you never will be married?"

"Not afraid, just aware. I'm not the sort of girl men notice. Since I grew up here, I doubt that there's a love match for me in this town, but the thought doesn't devastate me. I promise I will not accept Cleve because I feel he is my only hope."

Bobbie could see she had put her mother at ease. What Bobbie didn't know was that Maryanne cried herself to sleep that night. She couldn't even tell Jake what was wrong. He didn't press her, knowing that when she could talk, she would. As it turned out, they were both awake in the middle of the night and talked then.

It was wonderful for husband and wife to share how they felt. And Jake had to admit that some of his joy over knowing that his precious Bobbie had found someone special had diminished slightly. They talked until nearly dawn and once again overslept for church.

It was unusual that this should happen twice in the same month, but when it did, Maryanne always fixed a special breakfast and then the family had their own Bible reading and discussion at the kitchen table. No one was happy to miss services, but they all thoroughly enjoyed these family times in the Word.

After church Jeff commented to his father about not seeing the Bradfords. Bill seemed unconcerned and told Jeff that the Bradfords loved to go camping and possibly left after the work at the Micklesons.

Jeff had never known anyone who went camping as a recreation. He decided he would ask Bobbie about it in the morning.

eighteen

"I can't believe your whole family overslept."

Bobbie laughed. "It's not the first time."

"My dad thought you might have gone camping." Jeff said this thinking Bobbie would laugh at the idea.

"I wish," she said with feeling. "We tried to go my first weekend back but it poured."

"Where do you go? I mean, where do you set up camp?"

"We head east on the Sonoma Road. My dad knows a man who owns a ranch that goes back up into the hills. We camp in a wooded area of his land, near the creek. Some parts are so dense with trees that you stay dry in the rain. But it doesn't work if we leave the house in the rain and all our gear is soaked before we arrive."

Jeff was captivated. "What do you take in the way of gear?"

"Everything you need to survive the weekend—food, a change of clothes, fishing gear—"

"Do you fish?"

"Sure."

"Does Gilbert know?"

"I do now." Gilbert spoke from the doorway. "So when do we leave?"

"Not until I find out more about this camping," Jeff told him.

Bobbie could see that their questions could go on all day, and she knew she had to get some work done. "Why don't we talk at lunch?"

"I think she's trying to tell us to get back to work," Jeff commented.

Jeff and Bobbie tried again at lunchtime to talk, but Rigg came in. The conversation turned to business at the mercantile, and again Jeff's questions to Bobbie were put off.

Bobbie thought nothing of this. In fact she had forgotten the entire discussion, so she was doubly surprised when Jeff appeared at her side to walk her home.

"You can tell me about your camping on the way."

"All right," Bobbie agreed after a surprised moment.

"What do you usually eat?"

Bobbie was having a hard time understanding why this was so interesting to Jeff, but she was a good sport and answered his queries.

"My mom packs enough food for an army, but we fish and pick berries if the season is right. My dad always makes hot coffee and flapjacks over an open fire in the mornings. In fact there's nothing quite like an outdoor breakfast with a hot cup of coffee in your hand."

Bobbie's voice was so wistful that Jeff found himself wanting to try this camping business. He wondered how Bobbie and her mother managed in their long dresses but figured that was none of his business.

"Do you sleep on the ground?"

"We might now, I don't know. But when we were little we all laid our bedrolls in the back of the wagon. Don't forget, Jeff, I haven't done this in five years." The statement was completely innocent, but Jeff felt like she had punched him in the ribs.

"I'm sorry, Bobbie."

"Oh Jeff," Bobbie said as she immediately realized her mistake, "I didn't mean it that way!" Bobbie brought them to a halt with a hand on Jeff's arm. She could see he was still hurt.

"It's time we talk, Jeff," Bobbie said quietly. "I know it's suppertime, so if you don't want it to be now, then we need to plan on another time. You need to understand why I didn't come back for all those years. Otherwise I'm going to have to weigh everything I say to you."

"I think you might be right. Why don't you plan on having supper at my house tomorrow night and we'll go for a walk afterward."

"That sounds fine, and you'd better head back now because it looks like it's going to rain."

They were almost to Bobbie's house as Jeff agreed. Bobbie entered the house to find the family just sitting down. She had forgotten that Troy was having Carla Johnson over for the evening. Stuart, Alice, and the twins would be joining them later for dessert.

"Hi, everyone. Sorry I'm late."

"That's all right, we haven't really started," Jake assured his daughter.

Bobbie, who had been feeling preoccupied with her discussion with Jeff, found her mind moving to other things during the meal, the foremost of which was Troy's demeanor toward Carla.

Across the table from Bobbie, with her parents on either end, they were giving her a perfect view of their interplay. Bobbie felt something catch in her throat time and again over the way Troy leaned to hear Carla when she spoke.

Carla was a very sweet girl; Bobbie remembered her well from school. She had beautiful brown hair and it was obvious that Troy was devoted to her. Bobbie thought, with a certain bias, that Carla wouldn't find a man more wonderful than Troy, and if the look in Carla's green eyes was any indication, she felt the same way.

The meal began to drag for Bobbie. It was becoming increasingly hard to watch her brother in the beginning stages of love. Something almost resentful rose up in her over the fact that Cleve had never been as solicitous to her as Troy was being to Carla.

Bobbie immediately confessed the thought. It was unfair of her to judge Cleve in such a way. She knew what he was and it had never bothered her in the past that he didn't make over her all the time.

Even as Bobbie told herself this, she knew it wasn't entirely true. She did want someone who would look at her with love-filled eyes and who listened when she spoke because he believed what she had to say was important. But there was something else—something that Bobbie had not wanted to face. Bobbie wanted, no *needed*, a man who would be a spiritual leader in her home the way her father was. Bobbie knew that Cleve did not fit the bill.

He had admitted to her on more than one occasion that he had a hard time reading the Bible. And one time when they had discussed memorization, he told her he thought it was a waste of time. "After all, I've got the whole Book right here," had been his words, and they had bothered Bobbie immensely.

Bobbie often shared with him from the latest passage she had been reading, but Cleve never reciprocated. And another thing—she worried about his concept of prayer because of yet another conversation they had had.

"Will you be praying with me, Cleve? I've misplaced my spare set of glasses and I really want to find them."

"Honestly, Robbie, you don't actually bother God with those types of things, do you?"

"Well, yes," Bobbie had answered uncertainly. "I mean, whenever I need help of any kind, I go to God. What sort of things do you pray about, Cleve?"

"Well, not little things," he had replied almost defensively. "After all, God did give us brains and I think we need to use them."

Bobbie had thought on his words for a long time and did some studying in her Bible. If they weren't to call on God for everything, then why were the Psalms filled with pleas for help and praise to God for His every provision? Why did God state repeatedly that the very beasts of the fields were in His care if He didn't want his children to go to Him for their needs?

Bobbie ended her search with the verses in Luke 12, verses 6 and 7: "Are not five sparrows sold for two farthings, and not one of them is forgotten before God? But even the very hairs of your head are all numbered. Fear not, therefore; ye are of more value than many sparrows."

Bobbie had shared the verses with Cleve, but he had only shrugged, noticeably uncomfortable. There were times when Bobbie wondered how she could even entertain thoughts of marrying Cleve. Yet there were those occasions when he made her feel special or cared for, and she was almost sure he was the one. But the operative word was *almost*.

Bobbie knew that if she married Cleve, she was doing so with her eyes open. She didn't have doubts about his salvation, but Cleve did not seem to be growing in the Lord, and what was worse, he seemed content to stay that way.

Bobbie's beliefs were quite different. She knew the first step had to be an acceptance of the gift that God offered through His Son's death on the cross, but it didn't stop there.

The Bible said that when a person is in Christ he is brand-new, and it was upon these words that Bobbie faced the fact that she couldn't go on living as she always had. God was in control now, and old things like selfishness and pride were no longer to be tolerated because they were not pleasing to her Lord.

Some people would have said that Bobbie was some sort of fanatic, but Bobbie knew better. Never had she experienced such peace. It was indeed a peace that passed all understanding, a peace in knowing that her eternity was secure and that God cared about her every moment on earth, and was there for all her needs.

Bobbie knew she had to share her feelings with Cleve in a letter. He was quite sure that she would eventually be his wife, and Bobbie was having to face facts: Unless Cleve did a tremendous amount of changing in the time they were separated, she simply could not marry him and still be in obedience to God.

Maybe she hadn't answered her mother's question honestly. Maybe she was entertaining thoughts of marriage to Cleve because she was quite certain he would be the only one who would ever ask.

nineteen

Tuesday did not start well for Jeff. Sylvia was at the office very early wanting to see him. They hadn't talked for over a week, specifically since the Sunday before when she had left the churchyard in a furious display of dust. Jeff's several attempts to talk with her had availed him nothing. Three times he had gone to her sister's house and tried to see her, but she refused to even come downstairs. Jeff figured she needed more time and decided to back off.

When by the next Sunday Jeff had made no effort to approach Sylvia, her fury mounted. She waited all that day and Monday for him to try again, but by Monday evening he still hadn't made an appearance. Sylvia found she couldn't take anymore. Tuesday morning she was at the shipping office just after 8:00, dressed to perfection and wearing a forgiving smile on her face.

"Have you got a minute, Jeff?" Sylvia asked in her most humble voice, and Jeff, sincerely wanting to clear the air, walked her to the buggy.

"I'm sorry I didn't see you last week," Sylvia started right in. "I'm afraid I wasn't feeling very well."

Jeff saw her excuse for the lie it was, and for the first time he wasn't sure what to say to this woman he had been seeing. He was still trying to figure out what had been so upsetting about his suggestion that they eat at his house.

"Well, I'm glad to see you're feeling better now." Jeff replied with the first thing that came to mind, but he almost felt as if he had lied himself.

"Thank you." It wasn't what Sylvia wanted to hear, and she just barely controlled another show of temper. Jeff was looking uncomfortable, and Sylvia knew then and there that her plan had backfired.

She had deliberately let Jeff think she was angrier than she was, in hopes of bringing him to his knees. But all it had accomplished was to drive him farther away. The beautiful blonde couldn't help but wonder how long it would have taken him to come to her if she hadn't made the first move. She could see she had a lot of repair work to do.

"The main reason I came today," Sylvia improvised, "was to ask you to supper tonight at the hotel." Sylvia's voice could have charmed the birds from the trees. "Just the two of us in one of those cozy little tables by the bay window. It'll be my treat." Sylvia was smiling in a loving, almost intimate way.

"Thanks, Sylvia, it sounds great, but I've made plans. Can we make it tomorrow night?" Jeff was completely sincere and he smiled at her in true kindness. He desperately wanted to clear the air and even wished he could leave work on the spot to do so. But his talk with Bobbie was equally important and he knew he must not cancel it.

Sylvia was in a near state of shock. Time and again Jeff

had asked her out and she always made sure he knew her refusal stemmed from another man's invitation for the evening. But *never* had Jeff turned her down. In fact, Sylvia was tremendously prideful knowing that he dated no one else and hadn't dated anyone long before she came back to visit.

"You've made plans?" Sylvia asked uncertainly, and Jeff answered unsuspectingly.

"Right. You see, Bobbie and I need to talk, so she's coming to my house for supper tonight."

"You and Bobbie?" Sylvia's voice had gone very soft.

"Right. We should have talked when she first came back. There are some things which have waited too long to be cleared up."

It never occurred to Jeff to lie or try to cover up his evening with Bobbie. He saw the look on Sylvia's face and stood in surprise as she climbed into her buggy without a word. She ignored Jeff when he called her name and even shrugged off the hand he had laid on her arm. Jeff stood and watched her whip her poor horse into a frenzy as the buggy bolted down the street.

"What's the matter?" Bobbie inquired of Jeff, who had gone back into the shipping office and was standing by her desk like a man lost.

"I'm not sure. Sylvia wanted to go to supper tonight and I told her we'd have to make it tomorrow because you were coming over. She wouldn't even talk to me. Climbed in her buggy and rode away."

"Oh Jeff," Bobbie whispered, "how could you?"

"How could I what?" the young man asked in all honesty.

"How could you tell Sylvia that you can't see her because you're having dinner with another woman?"

"But we're not—you know." Jeff finally caught on and was looking at Bobbie incredulously.

"Well, *I* certainly know that, and so do you, but obviously Sylvia doesn't."

Bobbie watched Jeff turn from her desk and stare out the window for a long moment. When he was still quiet after a time, Bobbie spoke.

"You need to go see her and explain. In fact, I think we should cancel tonight so the two of you can go out."

Jeff turned and looked at the woman standing behind the desk. A wish rose up strongly within him that Sylvia was as understanding as Bobbie. But Jeff immediately pushed it away; it was a disloyal thought.

"Jeff." Bobbie called his name softly. He was looking at her but he didn't really seem to know she was there.

Jeff made an instantaneous decision. "Thanks for offering, Bobbie, but I'd still like you to come to supper."

"Are you sure?"

"I'm sure. I'll try to see Sylvia at lunch, but we'll keep our plans for tonight."

She only nodded, hoping that Jeff knew what he was doing.

❑❑❑

"Hello, Sandra. Is Sylvia here?"

"Yes, Jeff, she's here. Come in." Sandra was faintly satisfied to see Jeff on her front steps. She had just told her sister the day before that she would not lie for her again. Sandra thought Sylvia was crazy to have a gorgeous man like Jeff Taylor calling on her and pretending to be sick or out.

"Have a seat. I'll tell Sylvia you're here." Sandra walked up the stairs, glad to have an opportunity to show her sister she meant business.

"Sylvia, Jeff is here." Sandra poked her head in the door of her sister's room, which always looked as though a tornado had just passed through. Sylvia answered from the unmade bed where she had been crying.

"Tell him I'm sick."

"No," the older woman answered calmly.

"What do you mean no?" Sylvia's voice was shrill with panic. Surely Sandra hadn't meant what she said; she never did.

"I mean that if you don't come down right now and see Jeff, I'll tell him he can come up."

"You wouldn't!"

Sandra's answer was to shut the door and start back down the hall. But Sylvia snatched it open before her sister could move five feet.

"All right, all right," Sylvia whispered furiously. "I need a few minutes."

"Okay, I'll wait for you."

Sylvia gave her sister a withering look before slamming the door and rushing to the mirror. She stopped just short of repairing her face, a new plan forming in her mind. 'Maybe it would be a good idea to have Jeff see me like this.' Sylvia realized that she didn't look too bad. She touched up her hair a bit, took the last lace-scented hankie from her top bureau drawer, and went into the hall, her face a picture of rejection.

Sandra's eyes rolled in her head at the obvious display, but Sylvia's mind was made up and she ignored her. Jeff stood up from his place on the sofa as soon as he spotted the women on the stairs. Sandra smiled at Jeff as she passed through the room and Sylvia sat on the sofa and waited for him to be reseated.

Jeff didn't immediately notice that Sylvia had been

crying. He was too busy trying to find words to breach the awkward silence that stretched between them. Then Sylvia spoke first.

"Why are you here, Jeff?"

"I'm here to find out why you're so angry with me all the time." Jeff hadn't meant to say that, but was glad he did. He was, by nature, a noncombative person. He would usually go out of his way to avoid a fight, which included stuffing his real feelings deep inside, something that was often a mistake.

Sylvia didn't know what to say. He had never mentioned her temper before. She decided to go with that.

"You know I have a temper, Jeff. It doesn't really mean anything when I get mad." But the words didn't wash with Jeff and he again surprised himself by saying exactly what was on his mind.

"I can't agree with you, Sylvia. It does mean something. I somehow doubt that you would care to be on the receiving end as often as I am."

Jeff looked as vulnerable as he felt, and Sylvia felt ashamed. She felt instantly contrite and wanted desperately to tell him why she did the things she did, but if he knew how much she cared he would certainly use her; after all, that was the way men were.

It never once occurred to Sylvia that she herself used people constantly, with her schemes to trap Jeff into marriage, her sister and brother-in-law, and the men that she dated to make Jeff jealous. And in one sense Sylvia used herself. She knew if she ever got Jeff alone, really alone, she planned to use every wile in her power to get him to say he loved her or force him into a proposal.

"I'm sorry, Jeff." Sylvia could think of nothing else to

say, and indeed the words did not come easily, but Jeff was waiting her out, Sylvia could see that.

"I'm sorry too," Jeff replied, "if I've done something to hurt you. I really would like to go out tomorrow night. Is there anything I can say to change your mind?"

Sylvia stood and walked to the front window. 'So he hasn't come to say he's broken his dinner date with Bobbie.' The thought infuriated her but she fought to regain control. She kept her back to the room until she was sure she could manage a smile.

"Of course we'll go out tomorrow night. I shouldn't have run off. What time shall I pick you up?"

Jeff smiled. "You're going to pick me up?"

"Indeed. When I ask a man to dinner, I do it up right."

Jeff laughed with relief. It was awfully nice to have Sylvia smiling at him again.

Jeff had a quick bite to eat before he went back to work, and when he left Sylvia was smiling and waving at him from the door. To have Sylvia not speaking to him had been a dark cloud hanging over his head. It felt good to know that everything was out in the open. He should have told Sylvia a long time ago that it made him uncomfortable to have her so angry with him all the time.

Bobbie could see that Jeff's mood was improved when he returned from lunch; she was happy for him. Everyone's mood was light as they worked the afternoon away, and then Bobbie found herself between Jeff and Gilbert for the ride to the Taylors.

She hadn't felt hungry until she walked in the back door and smelled May's supper on the table. Gil assisted Bobbie with her chair at the table, and as she was seated a feeling of contentment rose within her. She had prayed a long time this morning and last night in regard to her conversation with Jeff.

As Bobbie began to eat she knew that God was going to bless her and Jeff for making this effort to clear the air and settle the past once and for all.

twenty

"Thanks, Mom."

"Yeah, thanks."

"Thank you for supper."

The words came from the men around May's kitchen table, and Bobbie was impressed. Bill had punctuated his gratitude with a kiss and Bobbie found the gesture extremely tender, but oddly enough, when the room cleared and she and Jeff were left to work on the dishes, she felt embarrassed.

It wasn't that she was unaccustomed to seeing shows of affection. Bobbie knew that she wouldn't have been embarrassed if Jeff hadn't been in the room. Why that was, she wasn't sure.

"Do you want to wash or dry?"

"I'll wash," Bobbie answered with relief, seeing a chance to hide her flaming face. Jeff had volunteered them for kitchen duty in hopes they could talk, but the piles of plates, cups, and pots were diminishing rapidly and still they had only discussed work and which kids from school were married and starting families.

"How did you meet Cleve?" Jeff asked suddenly.

"Well, he lives and works in Jenner and attends the same church as my aunt and uncle. We got to know each other when he started coming into the shipping office every day for lunch. Then he began to stop by my aunt and uncle's, and well, we just got to know each other."

"I must say, Bobbie, I'm a little disappointed."

Bobbie turned from the dishpan to look at him. "Disappointed? In what?"

"You." Jeff was actually teasing, but he was in for a surprise. "You don't sound at all like a woman who is head-over-heels in love."

Bobbie turned back to her washing. "Love is not the only reason to get married, Jeff." The words were said softly and sincerely. Stunned, Jeff had to tell himself to go slowly.

Jeff believed love was the *only* reason to be married, but something in Bobbie's voice told him that if he said that to her right now, it would hurt her deeply.

"I've always thought that love needed to be at the top of the list. What reasons were you thinking of?" Jeff's voice was nonchalant, not once betraying how fast his mind was working.

"Oh, things like companionship, wanting children of my own, security—those types of reasons."

"But not love?"

"I think love could come, especially if the two people care about each other."

"Does Cleve share your beliefs?" Jeff asked, still speaking with more calm than he felt. He was jumping to the same accurate conclusions as Maryanne had the night she and Bobbie talked in the bedroom.

"Actually they're more his ideas than mine, but I think they might have some validity."

"Might?" Jeff questioned her. "Then you're not entirely sure?"

"No, I guess I'm not. The truth is, Cleve has asked me to marry him, but I haven't given him an answer. He's coming for a visit sometime this summer and he thinks I'll say yes then."

"He's sure you'll say yes?"

"I think he is."

"And you?"

"I'm not sure one way or the other." They worked in silence for a few minutes as they finished the job.

"What does that look on your face mean, Jeff?" Bobbie was untying her apron and taking a seat at the kitchen table.

"I'm confused. I thought you stayed in Jenner all this time because of Cleve and here I find out you're not even in love with him." Jeff thought his words might have hurt her, but she answered as though everything was fine.

"I've only known Cleve for about a year. And one of the main reasons I've hesitated in saying yes to his proposal was because of how badly I wanted to come back to Santa Rosa."

"Then why did you stay away five years?" 'It's finally on the table,' Jeff thought. 'The question I've been wanting to ask for years.'

"You may not agree with me, Jeff, but I honestly believe I was in Jenner all those years because that was exactly where God wanted me." Jeff looked uncertain but kept silent.

"You can't believe how many times I planned to come home, but something always detained me. When I first arrived in Jenner I dreaded having to come back and face all the kids at school. My aunt was really sensitive to that and wrote, without my knowing, to ask if I could stay until Christmas. My folks said yes. Well, the studies were very different from what I'd been taught, and everyone felt it was best that I finish the year.

"By the following summer I'd made some wonderful friends and again my departure was put off. Then it was time for school to start and I was so torn I was miserable. You see, I still hadn't changed at all physically and I *so* wanted to come back—"

Bobbie stopped as all the pain she felt that summer crowded in upon her. She remembered the desperate desire to see her folks and the kids at school, but wanting also to mature and return looking like a young woman instead of a little girl.

Jeff was careful to keep his emotions off his face, but the look in Bobbie's eyes was almost more than he could handle. His hand clenched where it lay on his knee beneath the table, in an effort to keep from reaching for her.

"Anyway," Bobbie went on softly, "I told myself, one more year. But by the end of the next school year I'd begun work at the shipping office and my presence became necessary. The passage of time ceased to exist. I was needed and leaving was nearly out of the question.

"There was one time when I was ready to go. My bags were packed and I was going to catch the morning stage, but my Uncle Jasper got very sick in the night and again—" Bobbie shrugged and Jeff nodded in understanding.

"I did want to tell you, though, how much your note meant to me. When I first left I hoped you were suffering as much as I was, but I soon saw that there was no living with bitterness. It eats at you until there's nothing left of the original person and I knew that would be the worst thing I could do.

"The hardest part about being away was knowing that everyone knew. It was also hard not to hear from anyone. I realize, Jeff, that you weren't the only one involved that day, but I never heard a word from any of the other kids. Pastor and Mrs. Keller wrote, and so did you, but other than my family—"

"Not even Angie?" Jeff remembered how close the two girls were.

"She wrote but she never mentioned the lagoon. I think she felt that was best, but it's like having your mother die and everyone trying to pretend it never happened. I wish Angie hadn't moved up north so I could talk with her about it. I mean, I didn't need her or anyone else to belabor the point, but a word or two of understanding would have been welcome."

"I'm surprised no one else wrote," Jeff replied, "and now that I look back on it, I wish I'd written more than once. I thought about you an awful lot and I wished we'd kept in touch."

"Tell me something, Jeff. What's become of Richard Black? My mother kept me as up-to-date as she could, but she never mentioned Richard."

"His family moved out of the area about a year later. I don't know where they are now."

Bobbie nodded and then took Jeff completely offguard. "Okay, Jeffrey, now it's your turn. Tell me what happened with that whole outing at the lagoon."

Jeff looked shocked and then decidedly uncomfortable, but Bobbie just sat and watched him. He knew she deserved to know the truth, but he couldn't stand the thought of hurting her. He couldn't see any way out of it, so he looked her in the eye and started in.

"In those days I was seriously infatuated with Sylvia. So was Richard. I wasn't sure where I stood with her, and when Pastor Keller came to see me with the idea of the guys asking the girls to the boating, I grabbed at it with purely selfish motives. I planned on asking Sylvia.

"All six of us guys came here, and it didn't take very long for everyone to see that two of us wanted to take Sylvia. That left an extra girl, and that girl was you." Jeff stopped because he was feeling a little sick inside.

"Go on, Jeff. Remember, I did ask."

He took a deep breath and studied the face across from him. Bobbie became more attractive to him every day. But it wasn't just her looks. There was something wonderful and special about her to which Jeff was terribly drawn. Right now he could see she was trying to cover the vulnerability she was feeling inside, and once again he wanted to hold her.

"We hid in the barn to draw straws, which tells you how ashamed we felt, but we were too selfish to let that stop us." There was no reason to go over what happened at the lagoon; they both knew it well, so Jeff skipped ahead to when he dropped off Bobbie.

"I went straight home after I left your house and waited for my folks. They weren't long in coming and they knew everything. The church has matured since then, but unfortunately the gossip was pretty rampant. To say that my folks were upset would be a gross understatement. I've never seen my mother like that, but I had no one to blame but myself.

"I came the next day to see you, but you'd already gone. My dad went the next day to see Richard and Sylvia because I'd told him everything. He was very upset over the way you were treated at the lagoon. He talked with them privately and then left it up to them to tell their parents. I honestly thought they'd written you." Jeff paused for a moment in thought, remembering that at least Sylvia said she had sent a letter.

"Anyway, Pastor called all of us together to apologize too. He felt responsible. It just never occurred to him that there would be a problem; they were really trying to give us a special day."

Bobbie and Jeff stared at each other in silence. "I'm sorry, Bobbie," Jeff finally said.

"I'm sorry too, Jeffrey, for the years of hurt and scars. I don't harbor any bitterness in my heart, and I hope no one else does either, but it was time for me to hear the entire story. For that I thank you."

Bobbie slid her hand across the table and Jeff took it. There was nothing romantic about the gesture; it was a friend reaching out to another friend in comfort and caring.

Not long afterward Jeff drove Bobbie home in the wagon. Their conversation moved to Cleve again, and Bobbie said some things that disturbed Jeff tremendously, but he was in no position to offer advice to anyone on her romantic life. It seemed as though his own was in a constant state of turmoil.

Of course, he wasn't really sure that he would term his relationship with Sylvia romantic, but why it wasn't was a question that plagued Jeff until he fell asleep that night.

twenty-one

Sylvia was in her best winter dress for her evening out with Jeff. She had worked for hours on her hair after lying down for a full two hours to rest her eyes. Her dress was a deep sapphire that highlighted her eyes to their best. The nap was to ensure that her eyes were clear and not puffy or red.

Jeff was in a suit and Sylvia was very pleased that he had dressed up for her. He was, she admitted, quite the best-looking man she had ever seen. None of the rich men back East could compare with Jeff Taylor's tall, broad-shouldered physique. And if that wasn't enough, he had the most wonderful face. Very masculine, yet boyish when he smiled or laughed. His brown hair was a bit wavy and always shining with health.

Sylvia's head was raised proudly as she slipped her arm into Jeff's for the walk across the crowded dining room. They were given a table for two by a window. It wasn't really private, but the angle at which it was set and a large potted plant made it feel a little more remote. Sylvia had stopped earlier to reserve the table she wanted, and since Jeff was unaware of this, it confused him as to why the woman taking their order kept grinning at him as though they harbored a secret.

"So tell me," Sylvia said as soon as the woman walked away, "how did your evening go last night?"

"It was fine," Jeff answered easily. "We were able to discuss everything from five years ago, and I'll tell you, Sylvia, we needed that."

"In what way?" Sylvia always felt a little tense when the summer at the lagoon was mentioned, but Jeff's comment intrigued her.

"Well, Bobbie didn't know everything and naturally she wanted to, and I needed to know why she stayed away all those years. There was no anger or bitterness in either of us, but it felt good to get everything out on the table."

"Well, I'm glad to hear that. She and I cleared things up long ago. I wrote to her when she was in Jenner."

"You did? Did you mail the letter?"

"Well, of course I mailed it." Sylvia laughed as though Jeff was trying to be funny. "Bobbie wrote back, too."

Sylvia chatted on but she had lost Jeff. Why in the world was Sylvia lying? He wasn't sure how much of the conversation he had missed when he began listening again.

"And while we're on the subject of Bobbie, there's something I think you should consider, Jeff." Sylvia's voice had dropped and her face was a picture of compassion. "You know you spend a lot of time with her, and you want to be careful that you don't lead her on in any way. I mean, you wouldn't want to hurt her like you did before and—" Again Sylvia prattled on and Jeff could only stare at her.

"I'm not saying that you can't be friends, but you are very attractive, Jeff, and let's face it, Bobbie isn't used to having men pay attention to her. You understand that it's her I'm thinking of."

Their food arrived at that moment and Jeff was spared from making a reply. He found himself praying and asking God to show him what to do. Sylvia was lying through her teeth and Jeff knew that if he called her on it they would have a huge argument right here in the hotel.

Jeff drew a sigh of relief when the topic changed to Sylvia's family. She didn't have a good thing to say about them, and for the first time Jeff wondered how much of what she was sharing was true.

Jeff didn't remember very much about the meal or even what he had eaten, but an hour later they were walking toward Sylvia's buggy. Jeff was fairly quiet until he saw that Sylvia was not headed toward his house.

"I have to work tomorrow, Sylvia."

"You have time for a little drive, Jeff. Sometimes I think you're an old man."

Jeff fell silent under the attack, but began to feel increasingly nervous when he saw where Sylvia was taking them. They headed to a very quiet area of town that he had never visited at night. It was always talked about when he was a kid because it was said to be the place where teens in town went to be alone.

Sylvia pulled the horse to a stop beneath a huge willow tree. She turned to look at Jeff but he kept his eyes forward. There was a three-quarter moon and Jeff was well aware of the way it bounced off Sylvia's hair.

"Jeff?"

"What?" Jeff almost snapped at her as he tried to gain control of his emotions.

"Why don't we get out and walk around a bit?"

"Good idea." Jeff jumped at the idea in an attempt to put some space between them. Sylvia had pressed up against him in a way that was most distracting, and he couldn't get out of the buggy fast enough. He didn't help Sylvia step down because he didn't want to get that close, and he could once again feel her eyes on him.

Jeff was just standing and looking off into the darkness when he again felt Sylvia at his side.

"Look at me, Jeff."

Jeff complied and knew instantly that it was a mistake. Sylvia's eyes were filled with entreaty, and Jeff couldn't look away. When he didn't, she moved her hand to cup the back of his neck. Not until she had brought Jeff's head down and kissed him did he react. He stepped backward so hastily that he almost pulled Sylvia over.

Her voice revealed her hurt when she called his name in the darkness, but if Jeff opened his mouth right now, he knew he would be sick to his stomach. He had thought about kissing Sylvia, after all she was beautiful, but something inside him had frozen when he felt her lips on his own.

"Jeff." Sylvia's voice was no longer hurt. She was angry—furious, to be exact. She knew very well that Jeff had been waiting years to kiss her, and now she had practically thrown herself at him and instead of the passionate embrace she had imagined, he had stepped away.

"I'm sorry, Sylvia." Jeff's voice was hoarse. "This is moving a little too fast here."

"Is that right?" Sylvia's voice betrayed her anger, and Jeff's own temper came to the fore.

"Yes, it is," Jeff snapped right back at her, the inner turmoil of emotions emerging in one livid burst; he felt like he could drive his fist into the tree behind him.

Jeff watched as Sylvia stomped her way back to the buggy and then began to follow slowly. But he was about five steps too late. Sylvia slapped the reins and the buggy began to move away.

"Hey!" Jeff shouted. "Sylvia, get back here!" But the angry blonde kept right on going. Jeff stood for just a moment before he set off for home. He took the shortest route, across open lots and behind buildings, some deserted. It wasn't the safest, but he was wearing his good shoes, and if he went the long way around he knew they would be killing him by the time he walked into his own yard.

That, along with the fact that he found he had a raging headache. The only place he wanted to be right now was in bed, and as quickly as possible.

❑❑❑

Troy bent his head and tenderly kissed Carla. His hand came up and touched the softness of her cheek and he felt as he always did—that leaving her was torture.

"I'll come by tomorrow night."

"Can you come for supper?"

"I came for supper last night. Your folks are going to get suspicious. They might suspect that I want to marry you."

The words always made Carla smile, and that smile got her kissed again. With reluctance Troy pushed away from the porch and walked into the night.

The wind had picked up some, so Troy took a shortcut home. He was a couple of blocks away from his house, in a quiet area of town, when he heard a scuffle in the dark. The shadows were deceiving but it appeared to be three on one.

"Hey!" Troy shouted as he ran without fear toward the fighting men. His presence frightened away the attackers and Troy knelt carefully beside the man who had been left on the ground.

His face was turned away from the moonlight, but Troy could see that he was well-dressed and that the side of his head was a bloody mess. He had the shock of his life when he rolled him over and found himself looking into Jeff Taylor's face.

It was by sheer determination that Troy lifted the older man. Troy was huskier but Jeff was taller, and not a featherweight by any means.

"Come on, Jeff," Troy panted, "wake up and help me."

"I don't have anything," Jeff mumbled as Troy got him onto his feet. But the next instant he started to collapse, so Troy drove his shoulder into Jeff's middle and hefted him up onto his right shoulder. The dead weight nearly staggered him, but he pressed on. Troy laid Jeff on the Bradford front porch and threw open the door with a shout to his family.

twenty-two

The next hour at the Bradford house was like a nightmare. Troy was sent to tell the Taylors that Jeff was hurt and at their house. Jake went for the doctor.

The men had carried a semiconscious Jeff up to the first bedroom, which happened to be Bobbie's. Bobbie was by nature a pretty cool customer, but the sight of Jeff covered with blood was almost her undoing. The women stripped him down to his pants before the doctor arrived and then had only a few minutes' wait before the Taylor wagon thundered into the yard.

"The doctor is in with him now," Jake told the anxious family. While they waited Troy filled them in on what he had seen. When he was finished speaking Bill Taylor thanked him.

"We're just so glad you found him, Troy, and can't thank you enough for bringing him home. Nate, go to the Riggs' and let them know what happened."

"I'll go," Troy offered. "You need to be here, Nate."

The family thanked him again and then Bill went up the stairs to check on his son. Troy was back with Rigg just minutes before the doctor came down.

"He's got a hard head, May," Dr. Grade said from the stairway, "but someone tried to put a dent in it tonight. I stitched him up. His ribs are pretty bruised too, so I've got him wrapped. He was awake long enough to tell me that his attackers wanted money. He tried to tell them he had almost nothing on him and that's when they got rough. You can all go up but just stay a few minutes."

"Can we take him home?"

"No, don't move him. I'll come by tomorrow and check him again. He's got a concussion, so someone needs to sit with him through the night."

He gave a few more instructions and then Jeff's family mounted the stairs. He awoke when his mother took his hand. May couldn't keep the tears from her eyes when he tried to smile.

"Hi, Mom."

"Hi, honey." May's voice broke and Bill put his arm around her.

"My head hurts."

"I'm sure it does." Bill spoke quietly and just barely held his own tears. There were a million questions running through his mind, but he knew they were going to have to wait.

May was staying the night, so the men in the room told Jeff they would see him later. He was asleep by the time the door closed and wasn't even aware of the way his mother pulled the chair close and sat without taking her eyes from him, thanking God that he was still alive.

May sat almost without moving for nearly an hour before the door opened. It was Bobbie, and she whispered her apology.

"I'll just be a minute, Mrs. Taylor. I need my nightgown and robe."

"Oh, this is your room," May replied, startled. Now that she took a moment to look around she saw that everything was decidedly feminine.

"Bobbie, where will you sleep?"

"Troy has two beds in his room. We were caught off-guard or we'd have put Jeff in there." Bobbie stopped and looked at the man lying in her bed.

He looked strangely out of place under the white lacy coverlet, but Bobbie didn't feel like laughing. Her eyes flooded with tears as she looked at his bandaged head and wished she could stay and hold his hand for awhile. But his mother was here and that was best. She knew if it that had been her son in that bed, nothing could take her away.

The night was a long one for May. Jeff rested comfortably but May only dozed in the chair. Maryanne checked on her twice and even made coffee about 3:00 A.M.

Bill was at the house before 7:00 to check on his wife and son. He insisted that May let Gilbert take her home to sleep.

"But I want to be here when Dr. Grade comes."

"I'll stay. You're about to collapse."

Rigg knocked on the door just then and Bill was relieved. Rigg would be able to get May home better than Gilbert. But it was not to be. May was adamant and Bill knew he was going to have to see to the job himself. After a long discussion, it was decided that Gil would open the shipping office. Rigg needed to get to the mercantile and Bill would take his wife home.

Bobbie was very compassionate with Mrs. Taylor's plight but she did look utterly drained. Offering to stay with Jeff until someone came to relieve her, Bobbie found herself at Jeff's bedside a few minutes later. She carefully opened the curtains over the two windows in her room, since it was a cloudy day, and sat in the chair with her Bible.

Certain that someone was beating him in the head with a sledgehammer, Jeff's hand came up to push the pain away, but all he encountered was a cloth of some sort and more pain.

A small, warm hand grasped the hand he had put on his head and held it on the edge of the mattress. Jeff told himself to look at the owner of the hand, but his body wouldn't obey.

"Mom?"

"No, it's me, Bobbie."

Jeff didn't speak again but maneuvered his hand until his fingers were linked with those of Bobbie's. The act brought fresh tears to Bobbie's eyes and a prayer to her heart.

'This is my friend, Lord, and he's hurt. It's been so nice to have Jeff for a friend. Please take away his hurt. Please ease the pain in his head and side. Help him to know that You're right here in the room with him, and to know Your comfort. Help him to remember who did this, Lord, so they can be brought to the law.

'Please comfort his family, especially May. Help her to get some rest today. Thank You for the special family that they are, and thank You too for sending Troy home the short way so he could find Jeff.'

Bobbie felt much better after giving Jeff over to God. She was a doer, and it was hard not to be able to *do* something for Jeff's pain. And then the Lord reminded her that she *could* do something—in fact she already *had* done something: She had prayed.

Jeff wanted a drink about 20 minutes later and Bobbie found out what an inexperienced nurse she was. He did get some in his mouth but he also got some in his ear and down the side of his neck.

"I'm sorry, Jeff." Bobbie was not very happy with herself, but Jeff peeked at her from one slitted eye and managed a small smile.

"Are you trying to drown me?"

"I think so," Bobbie said as she carefully mopped his neck, ear, and then the pillow.

"Is this your room?"

Bobbie glanced up in surprise to see that Jeff's eyes were both open.

"Yes, it's mine. Is the bed all right?"

"The bed is wonderful, maybe a little short, but what can I expect when it belongs to a little person like yourself?" The words were said with a tired sort of tenderness that Bobbie found oddly touching. He had made the words "little person" sound like an endearment.

Jeff was drifting off again and wasn't aware of Rigg arriving to spell Bobbie. Bobbie took herself off to the shipping office with plans to check back at lunch. Business was quite heavy that morning so Bobbie didn't return home until almost 1:00. Her mother was sitting at Jeff's side with some mending when Bobbie appeared in the door. Maryanne set her work aside and joined her daughter in the hall.

"How are things going?"

"Good. Are you home for the day or do you need to go back to the office?"

"Bill was going to come in at 2:00 so I can stay here if I'm needed. What did Dr. Grade say?"

"He wants Jeff to keep still until he gives word otherwise. It could be a week."

"So he's pretty bad?" Bobbie's eyes showed her concern and Maryanne reached out to hug her.

"He's not in any kind of danger, but then he's not going to do any strenuous work for a few weeks either."

Maryanne went to the kitchen to prepare some soup for Jeff and Bobbie took the chair by the bed. Jeff didn't move for over an hour, so by the time he awoke Maryanne was back upstairs with a tray.

She helped him with the soup bowl and spoon and Bobbie went to answer a knock at the door. It was May, and she looked like a new woman.

"Hi, Bobbie," she said as she slipped out of her coat. "How's Jeff?"

"Mom is helping him with some soup."

"Okay, I'll head up and see if I can be of some help."

Bobbie followed May up the stairs, but only to tell her mother that she was going to go back to the office for the rest of the afternoon. Jeff was awake and grinned at her.

"You need to take some lessons from your mother, Bobbie; she hasn't spilled a drop!"

Bobbie laughed. "Actually I didn't *spill* anything. You looked a little hot and I was trying to cool you off."

Jeff chuckled and then winced.

"You better go, Bobbie," her mother told her. "You're going to hurt this poor boy if you get him to laughing."

When Bill found out from Bobbie that Jeff was awake and having something to eat, he immediately left for the Bradford home. Gil, who had been holding down the fort but was just as concerned as everyone else, questioned Bobbie about Jeff's health.

"He was pretty pale last night. How did he seem today?"

"He's still pale but he's talking and even making jokes."

"Did he say anything about how it happened?"

"No. And I have a feeling that's why your dad went to my house. It does make you wonder what Santa Rosa is coming to, doesn't it?"

"Yeah, I thought of that, but I also can't help wondering what Jeff was doing in that area of town when he was supposed to be having supper with Sylvia."

The two stared at each other, their thoughts running in speculative veins. It was almost a relief to have someone come in with a box he wanted shipped. Bobbie found her mind wandering in between customers, so she was thankful for a busy afternoon.

The lone shipping clerks walked to the Bradfords' after closing up for the night. There was quite a crowd there to greet them, but they were all family. Word had gotten out that Jeff was hurt and staying at the Bradfords, so someone from the church had brought over supper. Nate, May, Bill, Jake, and Maryanne were all sitting down to eat. Kate and Rigg bid their hellos and goodbyes, as they were just headed home. Marcail was upstairs with Jeff. Bobbie decided to eat but Gil climbed the stairs to see his brother.

❑❑❑

"Are you thirsty, Jeff?"

"No, I'm fine, Marc."

"Will the doctor be back tonight?" the petite child asked from the edge of her seat.

"No, Marc, he won't come again until tomorrow."

Marcail was nodding with relief as Gil came in the room. Gilbert scooped the little girl up and took her chair. He resettled Marcail on his knee and then smiled at his brother, who was regarding them with half-closed lids.

"Your color is better; how do you feel?"

"Sore."

"Has Dad reported this yet?"

"Yeah. Just a little while ago."

Gil wanted to ask details but was very mindful of the little girl in his lap.

"Would you like me to read to you, Jeff?"

"Thanks, Marc, but I don't think I can stay awake."

"Did you have supper, Marcail?" Gilbert wanted to know.

"No. I told Kate I'd eat later."

"Why don't you run down now? I can stay with Jeff."

Marcail complied and Gilbert settled back in the chair. He reached for a book he spied on Bobbie's nightstand but replaced it as soon as he saw it was her journal.

Jeff had fallen back to sleep and Gil was left alone with his thoughts. He wasn't usually a nosy person, but what had happened to Jeff was really bothering him. He prayed about how to handle the idea forming in his mind.

He made his decision before his father came to give him a break. After he'd had a bite to eat he walked Marcail home and headed to see Sylvia Weber.

twenty-three

"Someone is here to see you."

"Is it Jeff?" Sylvia stood up quickly from her place on the bed.

"No, it's his brother Gilbert."

Sylvia looked at her sister to see if she was teasing, but Sandra's face was completely serious.

"Tell him I'll be right down."

Gilbert had not taken a seat and he knew that Carl Boggs was eyeing him strangely. Gil spoke the moment Sylvia came into the room.

"Is there some place I can talk to you, Sylvia?"

"Sure," she answered uncertainly. "We can go in the kitchen."

Gilbert followed her to the kitchen and spoke as they sat at the table. His voice was kind and Sylvia responded to that kindness.

"Did you and Jeff have a date last night?"

She nodded. "We went to supper at the hotel. Why, Gil, why do you ask?"

Gil explained briefly. Sylvia looked almost faint when he was done. He opened his mouth to comfort her when she burst into tears and told Gil the whole story. He knew his face showed his surprise over the way Sylvia tried to manipulate Jeff, but Sylvia was too wrapped up in her tears to notice.

"Maybe I'm out of line to say this, Sylvia, but I don't care how angry you were. You had no business leaving Jeff out there by himself."

"I know that now, but I was incensed." The tears went on and so did more confessions. Gil wondered how he had ever envied his brother the fact that Sylvia had fallen for him. The thought of being such an obsession for this woman was a little frightening.

"I must go to him right away."

"Not tonight," Gilbert spoke firmly. "He'll be sleeping now. You could go by the house tomorrow. By the way, he's at the Bradfords'."

"The Bradfords'? What's he doing there?" Sylvia looked uncertain and Gilbert rushed to assure her.

"Don't hesitate to go there, Sylvia. They've been just wonderful."

"But why is he there?"

"Because it was Troy who found him and took him home." Gilbert's explanation seemed to put her at ease and he took his leave a short while later.

Gil was seen out the door by Sandra, who upon his exit went immediately to the kitchen. Both Sandra and Carl had heard Sylvia's crying.

"What's happened, Sylvia?" Her sister asked with genuine concern.

The younger woman was quiet for a moment before bursting into tears once again. "Oh Sandra," she sobbed. "I've done something awful."

❑ ❑ ❑

Jeff had a fairly decent night, with his mother again at his side. Gilbert was there first thing in the morning with his father. Bill again took May home and Gil stayed this time to sit with his brother. Bobbie, along with Nate, who had taken the day off from school, opened the shipping office.

Dr. Grade came by a little after 9:00 and said that Jeff no longer needed someone to sit with him around the clock. He also said he could sit up and even walk if he felt like it, but unless Santa Rosa experienced a heat wave, he was not to leave the Bradford home.

An hour later the house was empty except for Jeff and Gil, who was helping his older brother shave and clean up.

"I went to see Sylvia last night, Jeff."

"You did?" Jeff wiped the remaining soap from his face and looked at his brother in surprise. The simple act of cleaning up seemed to exhaust him, but he perked up at Gil's words.

"You might be angry with me, but I was worried about how you came to be in that part of town, so I went over to the Boggs' to get some answers." Jeff's eyebrows nearly rose to his hairline, but he kept silent.

"I couldn't figure out how you happened to be where Troy found you if you were on a date with Sylvia, so I went to see her and she told me everything."

"Everything?"

"I think so, and probably some you don't know. She said she practically threw herself at you to get you to propose."

"There was nothing *practically* about it, Gil," Jeff said softly and with regret. "She pulled my head down and kissed me." This time it was Gilbert's brows that rose as he gave a long, slow whistle.

"But you're right," Jeff continued. "I didn't know she did it to get me to propose."

"There's one more thing you should know. She's coming to see you today." As if on cue, the men heard a knock downstairs at the front door.

"If that's Sylvia she's going to want to see me alone, but I want you fairly close by because I don't think it looks right."

"Are you sure you're up to this? I can tell her you need to sleep."

"No, I'll see whoever it is."

❑❑❑

"You're angry."

"No, Sylvia. Honestly, I'm not."

"Then I still don't understand why we can't see each other anymore."

Jeff was nearly drained, but Sylvia seemed oblivious to that fact. He took a breath and tried again.

"Sylvia, I'm not going to be seeing anyone. I think my priorities have been messed up for a long time and I want to cut back on some of my social activities and rethink my purpose on this earth."

"So all I am to you is a social activity!"

Jeff's eyes slid shut in defeat, an action that Sylvia didn't miss.

"I'm sorry, Jeff, I didn't mean that." This time she was sincerely contrite. "I told myself all the way over here that I was never going to get mad again, but it happens so easily."

Jeff nodded and managed a compassionate smile. Sylvia reached and touched his arm briefly before pulling on her gloves.

"Well, I'll see you around," Sylvia said with a false cheerfulness.

"I'm sure we'll see each other at church. Take care of yourself."

"You too. And Jeff, I'm really sorry."

"Thanks, Sylvia."

Gilbert let a very quiet Sylvia out the front door. She had smiled and thanked him for telling her about Jeff, but the usual sparkle was gone from her eyes.

Gil stepped quietly up the stairs to check on his brother, but just as he expected, Jeff was sound asleep.

twenty-four

Jeff was remarkably improved by Friday morning and Dr. Grade said he could go home anytime. The problem was that only Maryanne was present and she had no way of getting him there. Jeff wasn't too concerned because he knew someone in his family would be by to see him and he would bum a ride home then.

Jeff navigated the stairs carefully and without assistance, nearly scaring a year off Maryanne's life when he walked slowly into the kitchen.

"Are you sure you should have done that?" Maryanne eyed him with concern when her heartbeat returned to normal.

"Yeah. I didn't try to gather my gear, but I figured you'd forgive me for that."

"I'll think about it." Maryanne teased him and Jeff saw instantly from whom Bobbie inherited her sense of humor.

"Speaking of forgiveness," Jeff said softly, "have you ever forgiven me for Bobbie's being away from home for five years?"

Maryanne turned slowly from the stove. She looked at the young man at her table and felt something stir inside her. When Bobbie first returned, Maryanne had known some very real fear that he would somehow hurt her again. Suddenly she knew better.

Breakfast was forgotten for the moment as Maryanne retrieved two coffee mugs and the coffeepot, and joined Jeff at the table.

"I'm glad you asked me that, Jeff," she began in quiet sincerity, "because it's obviously been on your mind. Had I known, I'd have talked to you a long time ago about it.

"Bobbie told me how well your talk went and what she said to you. And I have to tell you, Jeff, Jake and I believe as she does, that she was in Jenner because God wanted her there.

"I missed her, Jeff, more than I can say, but in some ways we were closer during those years than we might have been if she'd been living beneath this roof.

"But, Jeff—" Maryanne didn't raise her voice but her eyes grew urgent, almost pleading as she leaned forward across the table—"I need to tell you something that Bobbie didn't. She came to know Christ at Jasper and Joanne's. Now tell me, Jeff, how could I wish her back from that? When she left here she believed like my daughter Alice still does, that God would never send anyone to hell. And 5½ years is a long time, but Bobbie came back a new creature in Christ.

"Do you understand what I'm saying, Jeff? I forgave you long ago. What happened that day at the lagoon was awful, but so was what happened to Joseph in the book of Genesis, and look at the way God used him. And look at the way He saved my Bobbie."

Maryanne Bradford's eyes filled with tears and Jeff felt a stinging sensation behind his own. He had asked and she certainly told him. It was becoming more and more clear to him all the time why Bobbie was the way she was. There was no pity in this house.

"I too wish I'd come to you a long time ago, Mrs. Bradford. You've lifted a burden from me that's been weighing me down for a long time. I should have ignored my fear and come to you years ago. Thank you."

Maryanne smiled at him—a smile so like Bobbie's that Jeff found himself grinning at her. She had already had her breakfast, so after putting a full plate in front of Jeff, she sat and visited with him. It didn't take long for the subject to come around to Bobbie.

"I know this is none of my business, but have you ever met Cleve?"

"No. Bobbie has told us about him, but the only ones who know him are Jake's brother and sister-in-law."

"Do they like him?"

"It's hard to tell in letters, and I probably shouldn't try to read between the lines, but I almost get the impression that Joanne wants Bobbie to marry Cleve so she'll make her permanent home in Jenner. Has Bobbie talked to you about Cleve?"

"A little, and I can't say as I really like the guy, which is unfair on my part, but I can't get Kaitlin's face out of my mind."

"What do you mean?"

"I mean the way she looked after she said yes to Rigg's proposal. She was radiant, but Bobbie's not. She could be talking about her dog for all the emotion she shows when discussing Cleve, and I just—"

Jeff left the sentence hang. He wasn't sure what he would wish for Bobbie, and besides, he must have upset

Mrs. Bradford because her eyes were filled with tears again.

"Don't stop on my account," she said as a single tear rolled down her cheek. "It's just that I'm afraid that Bobbie is only considering Cleve because she thinks no one else will ever ask her." The words were accompanied by yet another teardrop, and Jeff, who had suspected something like this, felt he could cry himself.

"Is it true, Jeff, that no one would want my precious Bobbie? I'm sorry. That was unfair of me."

"I don't mind your asking," Jeff told her sincerely. "I understand how you feel. You want Bobbie to be loved. The more I get to know her the more I like her and want that for her too. But there's something very important missing in Bobbie's relationship with Cleve, and I can't get past that whenever I think of her married to him."

Maryanne used the corner of her apron to dab at her eyes, thanking God as she did that Bobbie had a friend who cared so much. Bobbie would be hurt if she knew she was being discussed, and Maryanne said as much to Jeff.

He told his hostess that he would be praying for all of them and the subject shifted to ways of making Jeff comfortable in the living room until his family came.

Maryanne gathered all of Jeff's belongings and was again visiting with him when May and Bill arrived. Jeff was growing tired so they bundled their son into the wagon right away and headed for home.

Maryanne changed the bedding on her daughter's bed and cleaned the room. It wasn't until she was done and on her way out the door that she realized she would miss having Jeff around.

Another thought assailed Maryanne at the same time, and she immediately wished it had never come to mind.

She took herself off to her own bedroom to pray. She stayed on her knees until she had given her daughter, Cleveland Ramsey, and Jeff Taylor all to the Lord.

twenty-five

Jeff was out of work for two full weeks, but long before those weeks elapsed it became apparent that the forces of law in town were not going to locate Jeff's attackers. An officer had come to question Jeff the same night he went home, but other than finding evidence of a struggle and a piece of fabric from Jeff's jacket, they told Bill there was not enough evidence. With so little to go on, including no identification of the assailants, they would have to consider the case closed.

Bill stayed in Jeff's room after the officer left and Jeff shared with his father why he had been walking home alone. Bill's face showed grave concern and then relief when Jeff revealed he had told Sylvia he couldn't see her anymore.

"I've been living for myself for a long time, Dad, and I think it's time I stopped. I could have died the other night, and I think maybe God used the attack to get my attention."

Bill had held his son in a long, unembarrassed embrace. They continued to talk for the better part of an hour. Jeff, having just arrived home, was very tired when his father left the room, but was also experiencing more peace than he ever had in his life.

The doctor cleared Jeff for work one week after he arrived home, but things were going well at the office and May asked Jeff to humor her by staying home an extra week.

By the last weekend of Jeff's confinement he was like a caged animal. It was Bobbie's half-Saturday at the office, and on Bill's request she agreed to go and see Jeff as soon as she got off work.

"Your father tells me you've begun to pace." Bobbie's voice came from the edge of the room and Jeff peeked over the newspaper he had been reading.

"I can't imagine what he's talking about," Jeff commented with extreme nonchalance. "I'm finding I could enjoy the lifestyle of the idle rich."

Bobbie spoke as she turned and walked toward the door she had just entered. "Then I guess you don't need company. I'll see you tomorrow or Monday at work."

Bolting out of his chair, Jeff raced across the room and pressed the door shut when Bobbie tried to open it. She turned and leaned against the wood, and then cocked her head to one side as she looked at the man above her.

"I take it you're feeling better?"

"Much," Jeff answered with a grin, thinking she was the most adorable thing he had ever seen.

"And perhaps you would like some company?"

"Are you going to make me beg for it?"

"Oh, now that's a wonderful idea. You could get on your knees and for once I'd be taller."

Bobbie put one hand to her mouth, her eyes brimming with laughter, when Jeff dropped to one knee and took her hand.

"Will you please tarry awhile and talk with me, Miss Roberta Bradford?"

It was too much for the small blonde. She dissolved into giggles and then followed him into the living room, laying her coat across a chair on the way to the couch. After they were seated together Bobbie removed her glasses to rub her nose. This particular action always drew Jeff's attention because she never complained about wearing them or said they hurt, even though it was distinctly clear they weren't the most comfortable.

"The office was busy this morning. Half the time was spent telling people that you hadn't been hit by a runaway stage or mowed down in a gunfight. It's been like that for days." Bobbie shook her head. "It's amazing to me how the facts get tangled. It wasn't like that in Jenner."

"You mean not everyone knew everyone else's business?" Jeff was amazed.

"Of course they did, but they had their facts straight." Bobbie's dry tone made Jeff smile.

"How are you at checkers?" Jeff asked a moment later.

"Fair," Bobbie said with a mischievous grin. "It all depends on who's on the other side of the board."

"Who do you usually play?"

"My dad or Troy."

"And do you win?"

"Now that would be telling!" Bobbie said, and then accompanied Jeff to the kitchen, where he set up the game. Jeff and Bobbie found themselves evenly matched.

When Jeff took too long to make his move, Bobbie would begin drumming her fingernails on the table. The scheme worked every time. Thinking she was merely distracting him, Bobbie was unaware of how drawn Jeff was to her beautifully shaped nails and exquisite small hands.

Jeff, on the other hand, found that nothing could distract his opponent from her move. She would cock her head in the way he found so adorable and study the board as if the checkers themselves were going to talk to her.

Jeff thought that if he bent over and kissed Bobbie's exposed neck, it would definitely snag her attention! Jeff suddenly sat up a little straighter. He was so shocked by the direction his thoughts had taken that when it was finally his turn, he just sat in flabbergasted surprise.

"Jeff-rey," Bobbie called in a singsong voice for the second time.

"Oh," was all he said, and Bobbie could see he was returning from miles away.

"We can stop if you're tired." Bobbie's voice had become very soft, and she tried to read Jeff's mood from the look on his face. He was staring at her so strangely.

After a moment Bobbie's hand went to her hair in a self-conscious gesture and then traveled to her glasses to finger the frames. Her movements pulled Jeff back to the present—the movements *and* the disturbingly vulnerable look on Bobbie's face.

"Well now," Jeff said with a shake of his head, his tone light, "I was certainly out of things just then."

"We can quit, Jeff."

'There it was again,' Jeff thought, finally putting his finger on the look. How many times had he seen Bobbie look at him with that expression of tender concern? But there was also a hesitancy in that look which told Jeff she was afraid her desire to help would be rejected.

"I'd like to finish the game."

"Okay," Bobbie agreed, "it's still your move." She wasn't at all sure what had bothered him just then, but his light tone told her he was either all right or didn't want to talk about it.

"Did Sylvia come into the office this week?"

"No, I don't think so—that is, I didn't see her. Hasn't she come to visit you?"

"No, she hasn't, but that's because we're not seeing each other right now."

"Oh Jeff, I'm sorry."

"No, it's all right. I've been burdened for a good while that I need to begin focusing on things other than my social life. It seems as though that's all I've lived for lately."

His words surprised Bobbie, but she didn't show it. She had been under the impression that he and Sylvia were quite serious, and now he had just labeled her under his social life. Bobbie was learning that there was really quite a lot about Jeff that she didn't know.

"I'll be praying for you, Jeff."

"Thanks, Bobbie."

Jeff won the checkers game and then May, who had stayed in the background during their visit, fixed them something to eat. Nate came home early from the shipping office and Marcail was with him.

"My birthday is coming up in two weeks, Bobbie, and we're going to have a party. Can you come?"

"I'd love to, Marcail, but I think you should check with Kaitlin."

"I already did. It's going to be here at May and Bill's, and Katie said I could ask whoever I want."

"Are any of your friends coming?"

"You're my friend, Bobbie." Marcail stated this as though it was the most obvious thing on earth.

Bobbie hugged her. "I realize that, but I just wondered if this was a family party or a party with a bunch of giggling little girls."

"It's a family party."

"Oh," Bobbie said with a disappointed face. "I really wanted to be one of the giggling little girls."

Marcail must have thought this was wonderful, since she threw her arms around Bobbie's neck and gave her a mighty squeeze.

Only Nate noticed how quiet Jeff had been through the entire exchange and the way he watched Bobbie. Jeff's eyes studied her face when she wasn't even aware of his scrutiny.

"Here we go again," Nate mumbled so no one heard him, but he couldn't have been too upset, since it didn't keep him from reaching for another slice of gingerbread and the pitcher of cider.

twenty-six

Bobbie went straight to Riggs Mercantile on her next half-Saturday because the next day was Marcail's tenth birthday party. She had wandered around for a good 20 minutes when Rigg appeared at her side.

"Hi, Bobbie, how are you?"

"I'm fine, Rigg, but I'd be even better if I knew what your sister-in-law would like for her birthday."

"Ahh," Rigg said with a smile. "I honestly think you could just bring yourself. Marcail would consider you gift enough."

Bobbie smiled. "I think she's pretty special too. How is Kaitlin?"

"She's feeling better physically, but she just heard from her father and he's decided to stay in Hawaii for at least a year. It was difficult to hear, but in the long run it will be easier than getting news with every letter that he's going to be delayed."

"I think you must be right," Bobbie answered with more knowledge than Rigg realized.

She had written to Cleve and told him how she was

feeling about their relationship. He seemed almost panicked because his next letter said he was coming to Santa Rosa right away. Wanting to settle things with Cleve as soon as possible, Bobbie had been relieved, but another letter came right after that to say that he wouldn't be able to get away until the spring and quite possibly the summer. It was a tremendous letdown, and Bobbie was discovering that the feeling of being in limbo was not pleasant.

"I saw Marcail looking at these last week," Rigg was saying as he pointed to some hair combs and ribbons. "And I know she likes lacy undergarments because she touches them and holds them to the front of herself every time she comes in."

Bobbie's interest was immediately piqued. "Does Kaitlin usually buy her this type of thing?" Bobbie held up a child's shift that was bordered with bright blue ribbon.

"I don't think she does. Kate's pretty drawn to that stuff too, so I think it's probably something they haven't had a lot of."

"Thanks, Rigg, I don't think you need to show me anything else," Bobbie said without looking at him, her eyes on the clothing before her. Ordinarily she might have been embarrassed to discuss intimate apparel with Rigg, but right now her mind was too busy figuring out what she could afford and exactly what Marcail might like.

Bobbie's stomach was beginning to growl from hunger before she made her final selection and started home. She was very pleased with her purchase and hoped her ten-year-old friend would be as well. She had only about 24 hours to wait before she found out because Marcail's party was right after church the next day.

Bobbie had checked with May about what she could bring for lunch but May told her that she and Kaitlin were preparing everything. The weather over the weekend would have been perfect for a camping trip but Bobbie told herself that she wouldn't miss Marcail's party for anything. She also asked the Lord to give them sunshine for the party. It was a selfish request, but Bobbie's heart was tender toward Marcail and she wanted everything to be just right.

❑ ❑ ❑

Just right were the perfect words to describe the day of the party. Marcail waited outside the church and then asked Bobbie to sit with her during the service.

Their pew was full, with Sean on the far end and then Rigg, Kaitlin, Jeff, Bobbie, and Marcail on the outside aisle. Bobbie and Jeff only had a chance to exchange smiles before the service began, but on the first song Jeff leaned to whisper in her ear.

"Why aren't you singing?"

"I'm trying to hear Marcail's voice." Bobbie's eyes were wide with wonder.

"You need to hear her when she sings with Kate and Sean. The word beautiful doesn't do them justice."

Bobbie was awestruck. Marcail's voice was the clearest soprano she had ever heard, and as Bobbie turned to watch her she could see that it was effortless. The whole morning was special and it was with high spirits that Bobbie made her way to the Taylors'.

❑ ❑ ❑

'You're going to have to face facts, Jeffrey,' he said to himself. 'You're finding Bobbie Bradford more and more distracting all the time.' Jeff sat in the living room of his house and couldn't believe he was having this conversation with himself.

The room was packed. Jeff's folks were there, along with all his brothers, plus Kate, Sean, and of course Marcail. Mr. Parker and Joey Parker were also present. They were friends to whom the family had a special outreach, but the only person Jeff had eyes for was a curly-headed blonde who wore glasses on her delightfully upturned nose.

Jeff couldn't believe how many times he had thought about kissing that nose over the last two weeks. Maybe it was because Sylvia had kissed him, but Jeff knew he was terribly preoccupied with hugging and kissing lately. He found himself envying Rigg, who had a wife to hold whenever he so wanted.

Jeff always assumed that he would marry someday, but lately it was becoming something of an obsession. He even found himself imagining what his and Bobbie's children would look like. He had never had such thoughts of Sylvia, and Jeff spent a lot of time asking God to show him what it all meant.

What if he *was* falling in love with Bobbie? She was committed to Cleve. Jeff found the name more distasteful all the time. And on the rare moments when he thought about Bobbie kissing Cleve, he felt something akin to grief. He had almost slipped one day at work and asked her if they had kissed much. He knew the question was none of his business, but it plagued him nonetheless. Maybe he should just ask her, get his face slapped, and have it out of his system.

The room had emptied while Jeff sat in a daze. Marcail had opened all her gifts and the family was gathered in the kitchen for cake. Bobbie noticed that Jeff wasn't present and went back to find him in a chair in the far corner of the living room.

"Jeff, are you coming to the kitchen?" Bobbie asked the question after she had stopped by his chair.

"Yes, I'll come right now," Jeff answered, glad for the diversion.

Marcail shot into the room just then and made straight for her presents. She scooped up the lovely undergarments that Bobbie had picked out for her and rushed over to Jeff.

"Jeff, did you see these? Bobbie gave them to me. Aren't they pretty?"

"Very nice," Jeff answered, thinking how grown-up Bobbie had made Marcail feel with such a gift. Marcail was holding up a cotton undershirt and bloomers; both were piped in pink braid.

"Marc!" Kate's voice called from the kitchen and the three went out together. Marcail skipped out to have her cake, thinking that this day had been almost as good as Christmas.

twenty-seven

"Oh Sean, not again." The words were uttered in agony and came from the 15-year-old's sister. Kaitlin had been sitting in the living room for hours waiting for Sean to come home. Rigg had sat with her until close to midnight, but he had to work the next day and Kate told him to go to bed. They were both too tired to give thought to the fact that Kaitlin had to work in the morning as well.

"Sit down, Sean." Kate moved toward her brother and then almost stepped back when a wave of alcohol fumes assailed her senses.

Sean mumbled something unintelligible as Kate put her arm around him, but she ignored her inebriated brother. Her pregnancy made her ungainly, and when Sean tripped on the edge of the rug, he almost took them both to the floor.

Kate wanted to rail at her brother. This was the second time he had come home drunk and she was just sick as she looked at him. It had all started around Marcail's birthday, when their Father had written to say he would be away at least a year. A few days after Marcail's party, Sean had gone out with friends on a Friday night and been gone until dawn. He had come back so drunk that his family barely recognized him. Now it was weeks later and it wasn't a Friday night, so they wouldn't have the weekend to recover.

For a long time Sean had been very sorry over what he had done and it looked to everyone like he had learned his lesson, but the boys Sean ran with were a strong lure, and in a matter of weeks he was seeing them again. He managed to keep this a secret for over a month, but now he saw them every afternoon that he wasn't working.

Rigg and Kate discussed the possibility of Sean working every day, but they knew that would be treating the symptoms and not the cause. Kate didn't like to think what was going to happen when school let out in two weeks. Unless Sean agreed to work at the mercantile, he would have hours of free time on his hands every day.

Kate was afraid to try the stairs with Sean, so she led him to the couch and helped him lie down. He fell asleep as she removed his shoes. Rigg came out to check on her just as she was covering him with a blanket.

"I could smell him from across the room." Rigg's voice was thick with pain. "How are you holding up?"

"I think I'll be okay. I came to some conclusions tonight as I was sitting here waiting, and I think I'm going to give Sean a choice; he can straighten up or I'm going to put him on the next ship for Hawaii."

"Will you be able to go through with it if he chooses to sail?"

"I don't know, Rigg, I honestly don't know." The tears that had threatened for hours finally spilled forth.

Rigg quickly checked Sean, tucking the blanket close around him, and then lifted his sobbing wife in his arms. The pregnancy made her heavier but she was still no problem for Rigg to carry.

He laid her gently in their bed and then crawled in beside her, covering them both with a light blanket. Rigg didn't try to talk to Kate as she cried against his chest because he half-expected she would cry herself to sleep. But Kate needed to talk, and after her tears were spent she spoke.

"I don't know what to do next. I love my brother, Rigg, but he's become so hard against me that I feel I barely know him. I know he's a different person when he's with his friends, and I feel that everything he says or does around here is a lie."

"It probably is. I mean, he's embracing the world with both arms right now and that means he has to weigh every word he says when he's here."

"What are we going to do, Rigg?" Kate said after a moment of silence.

"I don't know. I haven't wanted to involve my whole family even though I'm sure they've noticed Sean's behavior."

"But now you're thinking of talking to your dad?"

"Yes. He loves Sean, but he's not as emotionally involved as we are, and maybe he can shed some light on things for us. And just maybe, Kate—and this is something we'll have to face—Sean will have to make his own choice on this. He has a free will, and God wants Sean to come to Him of that free will."

They didn't talk much after that and it wasn't long before they were both asleep. Morning was a trial with so little rest, but they were up on time anyway. Rigg moved his hung-over brother-in-law to his own bedroom upstairs, and then left him a note telling him not to leave the house before Rigg returned at lunch.

❑❑❑

Kate and Rigg sat down with Sean that very night and talked over the options available to him. Kaitlin did not give her brother any ultimatums, but she did ask him if he wanted to sail for Hawaii. He was immediately against the idea and Kate found that she was relieved.

Rigg took over the conversation about halfway through, and most of what he told Sean echoed the advice he had received from his father that morning.

Sean was given until school let out to find a full-time job for the summer, not a job with Rigg or at the shipping office, but one where he walked in, introduced himself, and asked for full-time work for the summer.

"And what if I refuse?" Sean asked, not belligerently, but needing to know his boundaries.

"Then you'll find yourself out on your ear, because this is what it's going to cost you to live here this summer."

Rigg pushed a piece of paper toward the young man. On it were the weekly costs for Sean's rent and food for the entire summer. Rigg also told him he would have to buy his own clothing. Sean read the list over several times, and then looked into the eyes of Rigg and his sister. They were regretful, but serious.

Sean nodded slowly. He hated to admit it, but he knew he had no one to blame but himself. Maybe a job would help him say no to the friends who got him into the most trouble. Not that he blamed them completely; he knew the choice was his.

The next day being Friday, Sean knew he had just one more day before setting off to find a summer job. He thought he might have seen a sign at the livery. He didn't know the pay, but it had to be fairly high or else he would have to put in plenty of hours for his rent and expenses.

He also wanted to buy Katie's baby something special. She was due in about three months and he had put her through a lot. He thought if he could buy a gift for his new niece or nephew with his own money, he could prove to Kate that he did think of other people besides himself.

With this in mind Sean rose from the table to find Marcail. He had shouted at her today because he'd had a headache. Knowing he needed to make amends, he nevertheless wished his family understood him more. In fact, he wished he understood himself more.

twenty-eight

Jeff smiled at the sight of Bobbie on the step stool in the storeroom; she wasn't supposed to be up there. But then, it was only her boss who told her that, and since Bobbie saw no reason for the rule, she disregarded it when she felt it necessary.

"You're not to be up there, Bobbie," Jeff stated as he came to stand below her.

"Oh, it's all right. You see, Gilbert just had to run a quick errand and I want to get this done before lunch."

Jeff shook his head as she went back to organizing the unclaimed packages, even as his hands lifted to grasp her around the waist.

Once on the floor Bobbie glared up at Jeff, but he smiled engagingly, which only deepened her scowl. Sidestepping her, Jeff hopped on the ladder himself.

Jeff had been working on the back-room shelves for so many years he was sure he could do it in his sleep. As usual, his mind began to wander and this time it wandered to Bobbie. He had never had a friend like her, and indeed she was a *friend*.

It had seemed for awhile that working with her was going to be very difficult because of the way his heart was changing toward her, but he had fully surrendered his heart to God where Bobbie was concerned, and his heavenly Father sustained him in a way that Jeff never anticipated.

Bobbie had become his friend. It was really that simple. He could touch her arm or even give her a hug in true friendship. There wasn't anything they couldn't talk about. They shouted at each other once in awhile, but there wasn't a week that passed when they didn't laugh themselves to tears over something.

They even had a Scripture memorization contest going. It had been Bobbie's idea, and Jeff, having been raised in the Word of God, thought himself a sure win. But as usual, Bobbie surprised him. They would stand almost nose-to-nose and recite any verse that came to mind. The last person to say a verse won.

Jeff found out in a hurry that Bobbie was as competitive as he was. They were evenly matched at the moment, and both hated to be the last one standing there searching his or her memory for a verse.

"That's the lot," Jeff told Bobbie as he came down to stand beside her.

"Thanks, Jeff." As always, she had to tip her head back to see him. "I guess Gil was delayed."

"Well, no matter. Nate will be out of school in a week, and Dad always puts him in charge of the stockroom for the summer."

"I'm glad to hear that. Nate is fun to have around."

"Speaking of being around, I understand you guys are coming to supper tonight."

"Yep. Are you going to be there?"

Jeff gave a negative shake of his head. "I have a date."

"Anyone I know?"
"Penny Larson."
"Penny Larson? I thought she lived down south."
"She does. But she's here to visit her grandmother and we're going to supper."
"Tell her I said hi."
"I'll do that. How many more days until Cleve comes?"
"He'll be here Friday."
"*This* Friday?" Jeff was surprised.
"Yes. When did you think it was?"
"I don't know, but I just didn't realize it was so soon. You don't seem very excited."
"I am," Bobbie said, but her voice held no conviction. She met Jeff's eyes for just a moment and then turned away.
They had talked all about Cleve when Bobbie was still undecided, and Jeff had finally told Bobbie outright that her marrying Cleve was a big mistake.
"You don't even know him, so how can you say that?" she had retorted in anger.
"I don't need to know him to see that you're not in love with him." Jeff's voice had been gentle, and Bobbie couldn't take it. He had watched helplessly as tears puddled in her eyes.
"I'm sure you've noticed how hard it is for you to get into the office every day, Jeff, because of all the men lined up outside waiting to see me."
"So you are marrying Cleve because you think no one else will ask you?"
"You make it sound so cynical, but you don't understand." A single tear slid down her face and Jeff felt something squeeze around his heart. "Plain girls have dreams too, you know. We want families and homes as much as beautiful girls like Sylvia."

"Oh Bob," Jeff whispered, and reached to hold her, but Bobbie stepped away from his arms.

"Don't pity me, Jeff. I don't need your pity."

But Jeff was not to be put off, and he pursued Bobbie right around her desk and then pulled her into the storeroom so they could talk.

Everything had been cleared up between them before they had gone back to work, but at the time Bobbie's future was still very unsettled.

Bobbie now knew she wasn't to marry Cleve, but she couldn't tell anyone. She felt it a serious matter to tell Cleve first *and* in person, even though she desperately wanted to discuss it with her best friend—Jeff Taylor.

For the moment Bobbie was spared having to give any more thought to the weekend and Cleve's arrival because Marcail came in.

"Hi, Bobbie."

"Well, hello, Marc. What brings you in right after school?"

"Kate's at the doctor."

Bobbie looked at her with understanding. She and Marcail had discussed this before, and Bobbie, even though she didn't share Marcail's fear of doctors, was very compassionate.

"I'm ready now," Marcail said as she took a seat by the desk.

"Ready for what?"

"To hear about the camping trips."

Bobbie smiled. She had completely forgotten that they had been talking about it on Sunday when Kaitlin told Marcail she had to get into the wagon. Bobbie had promised her they would talk the next time they saw each other.

Bobbie glanced down at the paperwork on her desk and then at the clock. If she kept it short she could still get her work done. Bobbie was just finishing her explanation when Jeff came in and took the other desk chair.

"So when can I go with you?"

"Well, we're not going again until after Cleve's visit, but if Kaitlin and Rigg say you can come, then it's fine with me."

"What about me?"

Bobbie blinked at Jeff in surprise. "Are you serious?"

"Sure. I've been waiting for you to invite me all spring, but since Marc just came out and asked, I figured I'd do the same."

Bobbie looked from one to the other. Why had she never thought to invite them?

"Of course you can come," she said simply. "I'll discuss it with my dad and let you know what to bring."

Jeff and Marcail grinned at each other, and Bobbie was amazed to see how sincere they were. She wondered what it was that they both found so intriguing about her going camping with her family.

What Bobbie was unaware of was the way her eyes lit up when she spoke of waking up in a still forest, or going to sleep with a million stars shining overhead. She made cooking over the fire and hiking through the woods sound magical, easily capturing the attention of anyone listening.

The next day their plans were made. Marcail gained permission from her sister and Jeff asked his mother to fill in for the weekend. Bobbie was glad for something to distract her thoughts until Cleve arrived in six days. Before she knew it, Friday was upon her and the stage from Jenner would be in around suppertime.

Bobbie had the next day off, but she might as well have had Friday off, since she accomplished little. Jeff noticed her restlessness but refrained from commenting.

Around 5:30 Bobbie stood at the shipping office window watching the passengers disembark in front of the stage office. Her anxiety was overwhelming as she waited for that familiar face to appear. Finally Bobbie watched Cleve jump down from the stage, the last person off.

Taking a deep breath, she wiped her damp palms together and opened the shipping office door, completely unaware of the way Jeff and Gilbert moved to watch her from the window she had just vacated.

twenty-nine

Cleve spotted Bobbie the moment she emerged from the office, and he watched her approach. He searched her face, although for what he wasn't sure, and tried to smile as she came to stand before him.

At once he knew that staying away had been a mistake. He had been sure that if they were apart Bobbie would miss him. Not just miss him, but *long* for his companionship, as he had longed for hers. Her face told him that hadn't happened.

But he had a week in Santa Rosa, and he told himself that maybe it would be enough time to convince Bobbie Bradford that she needed to come back to Jenner.

"Hello, stranger," Cleve greeted her without restraint. It was so easy to talk to Bobbie.

"Hi, Cleve, how was the trip?"

"Long and dusty."

"I'm sure it was," Bobbie said with a smile. Cleve was so honest.

He didn't touch her. Even though Bobbie knew he wouldn't, she was somehow disappointed.

"Are you off work now?"

"Yes. Would you like to come in and meet my boss?"

"Sure. Do you work tomorrow?"

"No, I'm off until Monday."

"Good." Cleve looked very pleased and Bobbie wondered if maybe he cared for her more than she thought. At one time the thought would have pleased her, but now....

❑❑❑

"He didn't even hug her."

"What?"

"Nothing."

Gilbert turned slightly in the wagon seat to stare at Jeff, who held the reins loosely in his hands and continued to mumble to himself.

"What Bobbie does with Cleve is none of our business, Jeff."

"I know that." Jeff answered with a long sigh and then glanced at Gilbert. "But it bothered you too, didn't it?"

Gilbert didn't answer, but then he didn't have to; Jeff could read his thoughts. Jeff told himself again that it was none of their business, but his feelings for Bobbie made him wonder anew how Cleve could have kept from hugging her, even though they were in public.

"They're coming to dinner after church Sunday."

"Yeah," Jeff commented quietly.

"You were all prepared to hate him, weren't you?"

Jeff gave a small smile. "I guess I was."

"And it wasn't that simple," Gil remarked, and once again the two fell silent for the remainder of the ride, both contemplating the scene when Bobbie brought Cleve in to be introduced.

"Mr. Taylor, this is Cleveland Ramsey. Cleve, this is my boss, Bill Taylor." The men shook hands and then Bobbie introduced Jeff and Gilbert.

Cleve conversed easily with the men, his manner quietly charming. He was knowledgeable in the shipping field because of his close contact with Jasper and Joanne, and the Taylors were impressed.

Not a big man, Cleve was a few inches taller than Bobbie, with well-built, broad shoulders and a firm handshake. He was a perfect gentleman with Bobbie, and that was a plus for a man who had points against him before the game even began.

All in all, it was a good first meeting. Jeff did some serious praying as he settled the horse and wagon in the barn for the night. He was going to be seeing Cleve with Bobbie off and on for the next week, and he might very well have to say goodbye to his friend because of Cleve.

'Please, Lord,' Jeff prayed, 'help me to trust You for Bobbie's future. And help her to make the right decision.'

❑❑❑

"What *are* you staring at, Cleve?" Bobbie asked softly from her place on the front porch.

"You," he answered simply, and she felt her face warm.

Supper was over and the two of them were sitting on the front porch. It was a warm summer night and the song of crickets could be heard all around them. Their silence was a comfortable one, and Cleve had enjoyed just looking at the woman across from him before she became aware of his scrutiny.

"Did you want to ask me something?" Bobbie questioned him uncertainly when he continued to watch her in silence.

"I think I've already done the asking, Robbie."

Bobbie's heart began to pound. She had asked the Lord to help her bring this up at the beginning of his visit, but really hadn't had a clue as to how to go about it. Now Cleve had given her a starting place, and she wasn't at all sure if she was ready.

"Yes, you have asked, Cleve," Bobbie said softly, "and I felt it was important to answer you in person."

"I'm pretty sure I know what you're going to say."

Bobbie was quiet for a moment then. How did a woman tell a man that she was afraid she would someday regret marrying him? Bobbie was searching for the right words when Cleve spoke again.

"It's because I don't pray that much or read my Bible, isn't it?"

Bobbie thanked God for the opening. "I think," she answered carefully, "that people need to enter marriage with their eyes open. I mean, if there's something that makes a person uncomfortable, then he or she needs to understand that before the vows are spoken and not plan on changing that person once the wedding is over. Am I making any sense?"

"Yes."

"We've always been very honest with each other, Cleve, and I don't want that to change now. I'm not comfortable with the fact that you talk about love as though it's not important. I mean, getting married with the assumption that someday we'll love each other is not enough for me. But that's the way you believe, and I wouldn't try to change that.

"But the reason I can't say yes to you, Cleve, is much more serious. It's the exact reason you just mentioned." Bobbie's voice grew very tender and tears stung the back of her eyes. "God doesn't seem important enough to you, Cleve, and I just can't live with that. I know I didn't explain myself very well in the letter, but I had a reason. If you change spiritually, Cleve, it needs to be because of God, and not because you want to marry me."

Bobbie held her breath. The words were all spoken kindly and without judgment, but they were words that Bobbie was sure would make him angry. She was wrong.

"Thanks for telling me, Robbie."

Bobbie didn't know what to say. In fact, all she wanted to do was burst into tears. She had just hurt a man she cared for and also turned down the only proposal she was sure she would ever get.

"Are you okay?"

"I should be asking you that, Cleve." Tears streamed down her face as she answered. "I never meant to hurt you."

"I know you didn't, and the truth is, I haven't been completely honest with you." Bobbie looked surprised and he continued. "You see, I deliberately stayed away from Santa Rosa to see if you'd come back because you missed me. In fact, there wasn't a day that the stage came in that I wasn't there to meet it, always hoping you'd be on board." Cleve's voice was quiet, almost resigned.

Bobbie cried in earnest then. She took off her glasses and buried her face in her hands. Cleve watched helplessly.

"Robbie, please don't do this."

Bobbie tried to contain herself so she could talk with him, but the tears kept coming.

"I was really hoping you'd let me stay. I haven't had a vacation for a long time and I won't push you or anything—"

"What?" His words surprised Bobbie out of her tears.

"Well," Cleve continued, "it's just that maybe your parents would rather I didn't stay here, since we're not going to be—"

"You mean you'll stay all week, you'll really stay like you originally planned?"

"I'd like to."

"Oh Cleve, I was so hoping you would. But I was sure that as soon as we talked you'd want to leave. In fact I was afraid you'd even move to the hotel tonight and leave on the morning stage."

"I'd like to stay, and," he held up his hand as though making a solemn vow, "I promise we'll be friends. No hinting about your coming to Jenner."

"Oh Cleve," Bobbie said again, wanting to tell him she thought he was wonderful, but no words would come.

Bobbie had put her glasses back on and they smiled at each other in understanding. Cleve confessed to being very tired a little while later, and then took himself off to Troy's room, where he would sleep in the extra bed. Bobbie stayed downstairs for awhile to talk with her parents.

"He's awfully nice, Bobbie," her mother commented.

"Yes, he is," she said with soft conviction. "And he'll make some girl a good husband."

"But not you," her father interjected.

"No, not me."

The three were silent for a minute and Bobbie was glad that Troy was out with Carla.

"Are you all right?" Maryanne asked her daughter.

"I've been better. You don't mind if Cleve stays, do you? I mean, even though we're just friends?"

"You know better than to even ask, Bobbie." Her father's gentle voice was her undoing.

"I'm going to bed now." Bobbie stood and more tears fell. She was almost out of the room when Jake came up behind her.

"Oh Dad," was all Bobbie could say as she was enfolded in her father's embrace.

"You did the right thing, didn't you, Bobbie?"

"Yes."

"And you have peace."

"Yes, but I hurt."

"I know you do. God knows too."

Bobbie let herself cry against her father's shirt. When she pulled away he offered her his handkerchief. Bobbie shook her head and reached into her skirt pocket. Her own was so damp from her cry on the porch that she giggled.

Jake recognized the signs of exhaustion and turned her toward the stairs.

"Good night, honey."

"Good night, Dad."

Jake turned back to the living room, reaching as he walked to put his handkerchief into his pocket. His wife's face stayed the movement. He joined her on the couch, handed her the cloth in his hand, and pulled her against his chest.

He didn't ask Maryanne why she was crying, since he was sure she wouldn't be able to answer. But he suspected that it might have something to do with the light they saw in Troy's eyes in the last weeks and whether or not Bobbie's eyes would ever have that gleam.

thirty

Well-rested and ready to take Santa Rosa by storm the next morning, Cleve and Bobbie borrowed one of the Taylors' wagons. Bobbie took Cleve over every square inch of her hometown. Cleve was truly impressed.

"No wonder you missed living here—it's a great city."

"I think so," Bobbie said with a smile.

"I'm going to miss that smile, Robbie."

"And I'm going to miss being called Robbie."

They looked at each other for a moment and Bobbie silently praised God with a sense of wonder in her heart. It was miraculous that they could be friends after they had talked of marriage.

Their last stop on the way home was the shipping office so they could collect Bobbie's pay for the week. Bill, Gilbert, and Cleve became involved in a discussion as soon as they walked in the door, and Jeff, offering a ridiculous excuse, nearly dragged Bobbie to the back room.

"How's it going?" He whispered close to her ear as soon as they were at the back of the room.

"How is what going?"

"You know, with Cleve."

"It's fine," Bobbie answered, a bit puzzled. "We've had a lovely day."

"So it's going all right between you two?"

"Yes."

"When do you leave for Jenner?"

In the shadowy room Bobbie didn't catch the pained look on Jeff's face, but his voice told her something was wrong. She knew it was time to explain.

"Jeff, I'm not going to Jenner."

"You're not?"

"No."

"Why not?"

Bobbie brought her hands up to frame Jeff's face. He was bent over her and Bobbie spoke while holding his face very close to her own, thinking as she did that he was such a dear friend.

"Jeffrey, Cleve and I are not going to be married. But we are still friends, and he's going to stay the week because this is a break from work for him."

Even after Bobbie dropped her hands it took a moment for Jeff to respond. "How long have you known you weren't going to marry Cleve?"

"For a while now."

"Why didn't you tell me?"

"Jeff," Bobbie's voice was kind but very logical, "if you asked a girl to marry you, wouldn't you appreciate her giving you an answer before she talked to anyone else?"

"Yeah, I guess I would."

Bobbie looked away from him then, and Jeff realized how insensitive he had been in the last few minutes.

"Are you okay?"

"Yes." Bobbie's voice was nearly inaudible.

Jeff was not convinced. His hand came up to gently grasp Bobbie's jaw. He held her lightly and looked into her eyes. He saw pain there and something he couldn't quite interpret. He pressed a soft kiss to her forehead before freeing her.

As Jeff straightened he saw that Gilbert was rushing toward them. He appeared to be very upset.

"Honestly, Jeff, Bobbie's fiancé is in the next room and you're in here kissing her!"

"It's all right, Gilbert—" Bobbie began.

"How can you say that, Bobbie?"

"Oh Gilbert," she chuckled softly, "you're so sweet. Please explain to him, Jeff. I've got to be going."

The men watched her leave, and then Jeff explained to his brother, who promptly apologized for jumping to conclusions. They talked for a few minutes longer, and Gilbert admitted that he was relieved over Bobbie's decision. Jeff agreed, but kept some of his thoughts to himself. Mainly his worry over the expression he had seen in Bobbie's eyes—the one he couldn't quite define.

❑❑❑

"You better keep an eye on him, Mom. He'll make it so spicy that we'll all have tears in our eyes."

"Don't listen to her, Mrs. Bradford," Cleve broke in. "You'll love this chili."

Maryanne smiled to herself. She had never met a man who loved to cook. Jake and Troy were both quite capable in the kitchen, but they always preferred to have her or Bobbie do the work.

"Okay, Robbie, I'm ready for that pot."

Bobbie and Cleve worked well together in the kitchen, and Maryanne felt a twinge of regret that he wouldn't be a permanent part of the family. She quickly reminded herself that her daughter was a grown woman who had prayed long and hard about this man. She was not about to be an interfering mother!

The meal was wonderful. Cleve met Carla, who was over for the evening, and after the dishes were washed and put away, the four young people played a game.

When Troy walked Carla home, Cleve and Bobbie headed outside to sit under the tree in the front yard. It was another warm night, and the air was fresh and inviting.

"I've been thinking all day about what you said last night."

"What was that exactly?"

"That God doesn't seem that important to me."

"Cleve—"

"No, Robbie, don't say anything. I needed to hear that." He was silent for a moment, and then went on in a contemplative voice.

"You seem to have something that I don't. God seems to be very special to you, and I can't help but wonder why I don't feel the same way. In fact, I wonder if I'm even saved."

Bobbie opened her mouth to deny Cleve's words, but shut it again. She had no business telling Cleve that she was sure he was saved; that was between him and God.

"Is there a time that stands out in your mind as to when you accepted Jesus Christ?" Cleve asked the woman beside him.

"Yes, there is, a very definite time. It was after I came to live with Aunt Joanne and Uncle Jasper. Suddenly one night I was very afraid that I would die. My parents were sure of their eternity, but I wasn't and I wanted to be.

Uncle Jasper talked with me for a long time. I found out later that Aunt Jo was praying her heart out in the next room.

"It was that night that I knew I needed a Savior, and I turned to Jesus Christ."

"I don't have anything like that to look back on," Cleve admitted quietly.

"It doesn't happen the same for everyone, Cleve."

"I'm sure you're right, but that's not what I mean."

He was quiet for a moment, and Bobbie wanted to ask him what he did mean, but she stayed silent and prayerful.

"I've just always gone to church," Cleve began. "I've spent time with the people who attended church and I've tried to read my Bible and pray, but I'm not sure I've ever made that step. I'm not sure that if I died right now, I would spend eternity with God."

"You can be sure, Cleve. Right now, even."

Cleve turned his head to look at her. "I think you're right, Robbie, but after all this time, thinking everything was fine, it feels awkward to try and talk to God about this."

"He's the only One you can talk to, Cleve. God alone can give you a peace about your eternity. If you're not sure, then be sure right now. Don't let pride stand in the way. Tell God you know you're a sinner, and that you believe His only Son died for those sins."

Cleve was again silent for a moment. "I think I'm going to go up to the bedroom now, Robbie. Troy isn't back yet and I need some time alone."

Bobbie watched him stand, her heart aching. "I'll be praying for you, Cleve."

"Thank you."

The moonlight allowed Bobbie to watch him walk to the house, and as soon as the door closed she prayed as she told Cleve she would.

'I never dreamed, Lord, that he might not know You. Please show him, Father. He's searching. Please let his search end in You.'

thirty-one

Jeff ran his hand over his jaw and leaned closer to the mirror. He didn't have a heavy beard, but he did have to shave every day, and as usual he missed a spot on his chin. A moment later he wiped the remaining lather from his face and went upstairs to dress for church.

He was buttoning his shirt when he thought of Sylvia again. During his quiet time that morning, when he had read his Bible, she kept coming to mind.

After Jeff was injured he had missed three Sundays in a row. When he finally returned he noticed that Sylvia was not there. He looked for her the next week, and when he didn't see her he went to the Boggs'.

Sandra told him that Sylvia had gone to Ukiah to visit an elderly aunt. She didn't know how long she would be away, but when Sandra wrote, she told Jeff, she would mention his visit.

That had been weeks ago. Jeff hadn't given much thought to Sylvia until this morning. He couldn't get the thought out of his head that she might be hurting in some way, so he prayed very specifically for her.

With all of this in mind Jeff was not at all surprised to see Sylvia in church. She was quite a way away from him, but even from a distance he could she was very thin. He determined to talk to her immediately after the service, but when Pastor Keller dismissed the congregation she was nowhere to be seen.

Jeff decided to go and see her right away, but then he remembered that the Bradfords and Cleve Ramsey were coming to lunch. He would have to wait to see Sylvia.

❑❑❑

"Of course the Taylors won't mind, Cleve," Bobbie told the man standing before her. "And I don't mind waiting for you."

"No, Robbie, you don't need to. Just tell me how to get to the Taylors' and I'll walk over when I'm done."

"Hi," Jeff said as he approached, not realizing until he was on top of the debating couple that his timing was lousy.

"Hi, Jeff," Bobbie said quietly.

"Hello, Jeff," Cleve greeted him in relief. "I was wondering, Jeff, if your family would be upset with me if I stayed for awhile and talked with Pastor Keller. I don't want to be rude, but if you could just give me directions to your place, then I'll walk over as soon as I'm done."

"That's fine, Cleve," Jeff said, instantly sizing up the situation from the distraught looks of the people before him. "In fact, we have enough transportation to leave you a wagon." Jeff went on to explain how to get to the farm, and then Cleve said goodbye and headed back into the church. Bobbie would have followed, but Jeff caught her hand.

"I'm not sure exactly what's going on here, Bobbie, but if he doesn't want you to stay, you need to respect that."

"I know, it's just that—" Bobbie hesitated.

"Just what?" Jeff wanted to know, but Bobbie couldn't explain; she was too upset.

"Come on," Jeff said as he took her arm. He decided, for the moment, not to push her. "Let's find my dad and tell him Cleve needs a wagon."

Bobbie accompanied him reluctantly. She knew she shouldn't follow Cleve, but she felt so responsible for the devastated look on his face that she didn't want to leave him alone.

"Do you want to tell me what's going on?" Jeff's voice came through to Bobbie where they stood by the wagon waiting for their folks. She looked ready to cry, and Jeff thought he might be able to help if he knew the situation.

"Oh Jeff!" Tears filled Bobbie's eyes and she felt like all she did lately was bawl. "Cleve told me last night that he's not sure he's saved, and when Pastor Keller talked about Lazarus and the rich man this morning in Luke 16, well, I could just see that he was really shaken."

Jeff's face clouded with concern, and he put his hands on Bobbie's shoulders. "Don't you see what a good sign this is, Bobbie? You know how gentle Pastor Keller is. He'll know how to answer Cleve, and we'll pray until we see Cleve that he'll know before he leaves the church where he'll spend eternity."

"Thanks, Jeff." Bobbie's throat was again clogged with tears. Jeff gave her a hug just before they were joined by Jake Bradford, allowing Jeff to explain the situation about Cleve.

❑❑❑

"I've kept you from your dinner."

Pastor Keller grinned at the young man across from him. "I find I'm not the least bit hungry, Cleve."

Cleve returned the smile. He wasn't buoyant and he wasn't upset; he had peace, for the first time he could ever recall. He had fallen asleep the night before without really facing what Bobbie had said, only to be confronted head-on by Pastor Keller's sermon the next morning.

Pastor and Cleve talked for another 20 minutes and Cleve left with some key passages of Scripture to study in the days to come. He was partway to the Taylors' when he stopped the wagon and opened his Bible once again to John 3:16.

It had been there all the time; he could even recite it by memory. But not until this morning, when he looked into the kind eyes of Bobbie's pastor and heard him say the verse, did he really understand that it applied to him.

Sitting on the road with his foot on the horse's reins, Cleve read aloud: "For God so loved the world that he gave his only begotten Son, that whosoever believeth in him should not perish, but have everlasting life."

Cleve held the Bible against his chest. This verse was for him. He wanted everlasting life, and all he had needed to do was believe on the Lord Jesus Christ.

It had been rather simple, really. Pastor Keller had said a short prayer, something about confessing your sins to God and acknowledging that you needed His Son as Savior. Cleve had repeated the words after him, words that were from his heart.

"I always tell people," Pastor had said, "that if they *really* meant what they prayed, then they are now a child of God, but I don't think I need to say that to you, Cleve. There's something in your eyes that tells me this is genuine."

"I don't feel much different," the younger man had confided.

"Some people don't, but I assure you it's real. The Bible says to believe, and you do. Since the Bible is the Word of God, then that's all the assurance we need."

Bobbie had been watching out the window for Cleve almost from the time she had arrived at the Taylors'. She had declined dinner, telling her hostess that she would eat with Cleve when he came. So when he finally pulled into the yard Bobbie was there to meet him.

"Are you all right?" was her first question after Cleve's feet hit the ground.

"I'm fine, Robbie," Cleve told her calmly. "I'm better than I've ever been in my life."

Bobbie looked at him for a moment. "You're sure now, aren't you?"

"Yes, I'm sure," he said with quiet conviction, "quite sure."

The couple embraced, and when Bobbie stepped back she saw tears in Cleve's eyes. It had been such a painful time, one of uncertainty and hard decisions. But she would do it all over again, she told herself, if only to see Cleve Ramsey's face when he said, "Yes, I'm sure, quite sure."

thirty-two

Sylvia Weber was in a state of mourning. No one in the family had died, but her grief was just as great as if someone had.

After Sylvia had left Jeff at the Bradfords' those weeks ago, she had gone back to her sister's house, repeatedly telling herself she was going to control her temper for good this time. It was evident that for years all her thoughts had been of herself. What was further evident was that it had to stop.

As Sylvia rode home that day, her prayers were altered for the first time. Instead of mindlessly naming everything she wanted to, she asked God to help her change. She was certain that everything was going to be completely under control from then on, but Sandra met her at the door with a letter.

"I've heard from Aunt Velvet. Her letter says you're welcome to stay with her."

"Aunt Velvet?" Sylvia had asked in genuine confusion.

"That's right. I wrote to her and asked if you could

come and see her for a few months. It's either that or back home to Mom and Dad. Carl and I need a break."

Sylvia's lovely ideals about her temper evaporated, and she exploded at her sister. Even though Sandra looked guilty, she remained steadfast.

Sylvia had cried, even pleaded, but her older sister said it was time. Sylvia had left, but not in good humor. In fact she had vowed never to speak to her sister again, and Carl and Sandra were met with a stony silence right up to the time Sylvia boarded the stage.

Sandra, terribly guilt-ridden, had written to her the very day she left and every few days in the coming weeks. Sylvia, however, didn't reply. Worried that something had happened to her spoiled sister, Sandra finally received a letter from Sylvia almost a month after her departure.

She had said little, but Sandra began to sense a change in her. What Sandra didn't know was that Sylvia had met an older version of herself: Aunt Velvet. It was enough to send Sylvia into a near state of shock.

Sylvia had never met her Aunt Velvet, and never really believed all the stories she had heard about her. But they were all too true. The older woman had never married, although she must have been a beauty in her day, and Sylvia quickly found out why: There was no living with her. Not a minute passed when she didn't insist on having something her own way.

If it wasn't a fit about Sylvia not taking the teacup with the chip in it, it was the silent treatment because her niece had dared to disagree with her over some trivial matter.

Aunt Velvet had little money, but she tried to live like a queen. She owed people all over town, and Sylvia was mortified when the shopkeepers in town would look at her lovely clothes and pull out an invoice from behind the counter. "Can you pay your aunt's bill?"

Sylvia heard the words so many times that she dreamt about them. In short, her aunt was held in contempt by the community, and to be associated with her was far and away the most humiliating thing Sylvia had ever experienced.

That Sylvia was headed in the same direction occurred to her one morning before her aunt arose. Standing in the living room of Velvet's ramshackle house, Sylvia looked at the possessions of a woman who never cared about anyone but herself.

On every wall there was a mirror, sometimes two. Keepsakes from days gone by lined the shelves, little mementos that Aunt Velvet must have received from the men who had courted and tried to woo her.

Tears streamed down Sylvia's face when she thought of her bedroom at Sandra's home. On the dresser was a dried-up flower that Jeff had given her months ago, and beside it was a torn page that had fallen from his Bible one day in church. Sylvia had taken it without telling him for a keepsake, and now felt ashamed.

That day Sylvia wrote and asked Sandra if she could come back. Sandra had not immediately acquiesced, and Sylvia had been miserable. Sylvia asked in every letter to Sandra when she could return. Finally a letter arrived telling Sylvia she would be welcome. She had packed her things and left that very day.

Sylvia still had Sandra's letter that told of Jeff's visit, but she didn't hold out any hope for the future. Her return to Santa Rosa was not to see Jeff, although she would love to talk with him. No, her return to Santa Rosa was to put some space between her and Aunt Velvet so she could mourn in private—mourn for the 20-plus years spent living for herself and accomplishing nothing for God and in reality nothing for herself.

Sylvia stayed away from church the first Sunday back, feeling that she still needed some time to think. On the Sunday she did attend, it caused her almost a physical pain to see Jeff talking so easily with Bobbie Bradford, but it didn't make her angry.

Several people came right out and asked Sylvia if she had been ill, making her uncomfortably aware of how thin she had become. Her pride came to the fore over this matter, and she didn't stay after church because she didn't want Jeff to see her.

Surprisingly enough, though, she was not at all upset when Jeff came to the house that night. In fact, she was so glad to see him she had to swallow hard against the lump in her throat.

"Hello, Jeff."

"Hello, yourself. Welcome back."

"Thanks."

Sylvia motioned him to a seat in the living room and sat across from him.

"I was all ready to ask how you were doing, but I think I can see you're okay." The words were said kindly, and Sylvia realized Jeff was looking at her eyes, and not the way her dress hung on her frame.

"I am doing okay. How about yourself?"

"I'm fine. How was your visit with your aunt?"

"Interesting," Sylvia said, and then smiled. Jeff smiled back and wondered at the emotional change in her.

To look at her one would think she had been quite ill, but her eyes belied the frail look of her body. Those big sapphire-blue orbs looked out with a guileless serenity that Jeff had never seen there before.

They talked for over an hour, and as Jeff was ready to leave, something compelled him to ask Sylvia out.

"Maybe we could go to supper sometime."

"Oh, I'd like that, Jeff," Sylvia answered, her eyes shining with pleasure.

"Great! How's Thursday night?"

"Thursday is fine."

"Okay, I'll stop by about 6:30. See you then."

"Good night, Jeff." Sylvia stood at the front door and watched until he was out of sight. She begged God to help her keep her heart in check. But Jeff Taylor was a wonderful man and Sylvia had always been a little bit in love with him. She wasn't sure it was possible to see him socially and not fall for him all over again.

Sylvia recognized the fact that there weren't many men who would still be friendly with her after the way she had acted. In fact, she meant to apologize about that. Thursday night, she told herself, as she went into the kitchen to tell Sandra she had a date.

thirty-three

The week flew by and Cleve could hardly believe he was leaving town the next day. He had a wonderful time with Bobbie, and praised God for her spiritual influence and the opportunity to come and see her.

Cleve had gone every day to the shipping office to eat lunch with Bobbie and the Taylor sons, and every day he wondered the same thing: How long would it be before Jeff and Bobbie knew they were in love?

Strangely enough, he was not jealous, but to him the way they cared for each other would have been obvious to a blind man: their specific smiles for each other with which no one else was gifted. Private jokes, although shared with everyone, nevertheless singled them out as something special.

Their last lunch together was at the hotel on Thursday, before Cleve would be taking the morning stage home. Bobbie announced she would treat.

"Have you fallen into a large sum of money?" Jeff wanted to know.

"It's impolite," Bobbie informed him with her nose in the air, "to ask a lady about her age, weight, or bank account." Bobbie said this with the snootiest voice she could muster.

"Is that right?"

"Yes, that's right, and anyone who's anyone would certainly know that."

"Well, I know your age and I would guess that your weight is somewhere in the neighborhood of a hundred pounds soaking wet, but your bank account, now that's a mystery." Jeff wagged his finger under her nose and tried to look stern.

"Get that finger any closer and I'll bite it," she promised him.

Cleve could only shake his head. They played around like sweethearts. Even the fact that Jeff had a date with another woman that night couldn't change Cleve's mind. Too many times he had seen Jeff drop his arm protectively around Bobbie's shoulders, and even kiss her cheek or forehead. Brothers and sisters wouldn't have acted this way.

Cleve knew that Bobbie considered Jeff a friend, and vice versa, but Cleve believed these two were on the threshold of something far more intimate. He said as much to Mrs. Taylor the night before he left town.

"Yes, Cleve, I have noticed that they have a very close relationship. Jeff is going camping with Jake and the kids the weekend after this, and something tells me things might come to a boil," Maryanne shrugged noncommittally. "But then I've been wrong before."

❑❑❑

"Honestly, Cleve, this has been some kind of a miracle—I mean your coming here and talking with Pastor Keller."

"Yeah," he agreed with a smile.

Every evening Bobbie and Cleve had spent time in the Word. Bible lessons that had been no more than stories to Cleve now had personal application. The look of wonder, and often conviction, that Bobbie saw on his face was at once joyful and sobering.

"I'll be praying for you, Cleveland."

"And I'll be praying for you." They hugged each other, and Cleve told her how excited he was to go home and tell Jasper and Joanne of his salvation.

"Give them my love."

Jeff and Gil came from the shipping office just as the stage arrived, and all the men shook hands. Jeff's arm dropped around Bobbie's shoulders in a familiar fashion and that was the last sight Cleve had of Bobbie as the stage pulled out of town.

"How long, Lord?" Cleve said inside the empty stage. "How long before they discover their true feelings for each other?"

thirty-four

Things did not "come to a boil," as Maryanne had predicted, but Jeff did find out in a hurry that what he had always suspected was true: Going camping with the Bradfords was going to be fun!

Marcail shared his feelings and was in the shipping office every day to question Bobbie.

"Bobbie, did you get my bedroll all set?"

"I sure did. We're going to sleep in the back of the wagon and we'll share the blankets."

"How about Jeff's?"

"Good question, how about Jeff's?" Jeff asked as he joined the ladies at the desk. He was equally as excited and did nothing to hide it.

"We've got you all set too," Bobbie told him with an indulgent smile that might not have been as well-received if he hadn't been so enthusiastic about this outdoor excursion.

"Now let me get this straight," Jeff questioned her for at least the tenth time. "We leave Friday at about 5:00 and we have an hour, maybe an hour-and-a-half, before we reach the place where we camp."

"Right." Bobbie couldn't hide her smile. He was so much fun to watch. Of course she remembered acting the same way when her father had first taken her and Troy. They must have driven him nuts with their nonstop questions and chatter. Jeff and Marcail were almost as bad.

Everyone planned to meet at the Bradfords', with the exception of Sean, who usually worked until 6:00 at the livery. Joey Parker came with Kaitlin and Rigg to see Marcail off, and Bobbie thought he was the sweetest little boy she had ever encountered. But her attention didn't linger on Joey for very long as she watched Kate, thinking that she looked tired and uncomfortable.

Bobbie's eyes misted just a bit when Rigg helped her down from the wagon with extreme care, but then she felt like giggling at the way Kate waddled, her stomach going before her like the prow of a ship. Kate stopped in front of Bobbie and the younger woman couldn't hide her grin.

"I walk like a duck, don't I?"

Bobbie's hand covered her mouth, but her eyes told Kate she was about to laugh. "I'm sorry, Kaitlin."

Kate smiled. "Don't apologize. You can't do anything that Rigg hasn't done already, including quack like a duck when he walks behind me."

"He really does that?"

"Well, he did. But one day I burst into tears and he stopped." Kate gave a mighty sigh. "A man thinks he knows the woman he's married, but then she gets pregnant and cries for no reason, or craves fried chicken at three in the morning. And the heat—it's enough to drive me crazy!"

"This isn't a very hot summer."

"It is if you're pregnant," Kate assured her.

Bobbie nodded, remembering that Alice had said something about that as well.

"We're all set," Jake called from his place beside the wagon.

Bobbie watched Marcail hug her sister. "You listen and obey Marc," Kate told her. "Stay close to the others so they don't lose you."

"I will." Marcail was squirming with excitement, making Kate laugh. Rigg snatched her close for an instant when it looked like she had forgotten to hug him, and they all watched as she scrambled into the back of the wagon.

Jeff was talking with Maryanne as Bobbie climbed aboard, and she heard part of their conversation.

"I just assumed that the whole family went."

"I've never cared for camping and I'm also a person who loves solitude, so I don't mind having the house to myself for an entire weekend."

She grinned at Jeff before moving to kiss her son and daughter goodbye, and then she went to her husband. Jake wrapped her in his arms and they kissed, unembarrassed, for a long time. He whispered something in Maryanne's ear that made her smile and then took his seat and picked up the reins.

They were waved out of the yard with smiles and laughter, and when Bobbie turned back to settle in for the ride, she found both Jeff and Marcail staring at her from their places nearby in the back of the wagon.

"What?" Bobbie asked with a raised brow.

"Nothing." Jeff answered as they both kept smiling.

Bobbie shook her head and thanked the Lord for these good friends. She also prayed that this weekend would be all that they hoped it would be.

❑❑❑

One hour and twenty minutes later Jake brought the wagon to a stop under a huge oak tree. The creek was in plain view some 30 feet away, and the sound it made as it tripped lightly over the rock-filled bed was immediately comforting to Bobbie.

Jake and Troy went to work setting up camp, and Jeff also pitched in, doing with quiet efficiency whatever he was instructed. Bobbie and Marcail had disappeared somewhere and Jeff figured they were collecting firewood.

Camp was swiftly put into shape, with bedrolls, fishing tackle, provisions box, and rain ponchos all unloaded. They were stacked neatly under the wagon or next to the huge logs that were laid out in a triangle around the spot where the fire would be built.

It was during the building of the fire that Jeff became confused. Troy appeared at his side with an armful of logs.

"Where are Bobbie and Marc?"

"Oh, they probably went to change," Troy told him nonchalantly, and even though Jeff was unsure what he meant, he didn't need to ask because the girls materialized at that moment, both wearing pants.

Troy headed back into the surrounding woods and Jeff was left staring at the girls as they put their other clothing under the wagon seat. Jake's voice came low to his ears from where he had come close with his own armload of wood.

"I've been getting jeans for Bob to wear camping since she was a little girl," Jake began, having seen the look on the younger man's face. "She's always very discreet about it and Bobbie asked Kaitlin's permission before she found some for Marcail. But, Jeff," Jake stopped until he was sure he had his attention, "if you're offended, Bobbie can go and change right now."

Jeff's gaze swung once again to the girls. Bobbie's pants were very baggy, and in fact he could only see them from the knees down because of the oversized man's shirt she was wearing. Marcail's shirt stopped just below her hips, and she would have looked like a boy standing there if it weren't for the fat black braid that hung down her back.

"No, she doesn't need to change, although I appreciate your giving me a moment to get used to the idea."

Jake's look was understanding as he asked Jeff to build the fire. Thinking he had put a strain on the evening, Jeff was grateful for something to do.

Bobbie and Marcail were as ladylike as always, and supper was a mixture of delicious food and laughter. They used the provisions from home for that meal, but Troy and Jake set out snares for the meals the following day. Bobbie planned to be up early to do some fishing. Jeff told himself he would join her, but she and Troy left camp so quietly that Jeff and Marcail slept through it.

❑❑❑

Brother and sister sat side-by-side on the creek bank and talked in low tones.

"I thought Carla was going to come this weekend," Bobbie commented just as she felt a tug on her line. Troy didn't answer for a minute because his mind was still working on the fact that Bobbie hadn't lost her touch. She was one of the best anglers he knew.

"It's her dad's birthday and they're having a special dinner tonight."

"Why didn't you stay?"

Troy chuckled softly. "I love Carla, but I'd much rather go camping than attend a birthday party."

Tears flooded Bobbie's eyes when her brother confided that he loved his girlfriend. She turned her face quickly back to the water, but Troy noticed.

"What's the matter?"

"Nothing."

"You like Carla, don't you?"

"Oh Troy, she's wonderful! Please don't mind me."

They were quiet for a moment. Two more fish were snagged, one for each of them, and then Troy spoke quietly.

"I liked Cleve."

"I like him too, Troy, but *like* isn't enough to build a marriage on."

"No, I guess it isn't."

"Are you and Carla going to be married?"

"Yes."

"What are you waiting for?"

"I want to put a little money away."

"How does Carla feel about that?"

"She wants to be married right away. She says she can go to work if we need the money, but I don't want my wife working."

"Oh, I can see why you must feel that way. Your own mother has worked out of the house for years, and you can see how miserable she and Dad are." Bobbie's voice was sarcastic in the extreme, and Troy just stared at her.

"And of course," she went on relentlessly, "it's much easier to say goodbye to your future wife on her parents' front porch than in the privacy of your own home where you can hold her all you want."

"Well, I guess you told me," Troy muttered good-naturedly, but Bobbie could see her words had affected him. They were quiet again while Bobbie brought in three more fish in quick succession.

"How do you do that?" Troy asked in some exasperation, but she only laughed. They talked on in close companionship for another few minutes before they were joined by Jeff.

He was unshaven and a little fuzzy around the edges. Bobbie didn't think she had ever seen him look so cute.

"Good morning," Troy greeted him.

"Hi." His voice was gravelly from lack of use.

Bobbie smiled. "How did you sleep?"

"It took me awhile to fall asleep, but once I went out, it was for the night." Jeff rubbed his back and Bobbie asked what was wrong.

"I think I missed one of the rocks under my bedroll, and it left a permanent dent in my back."

Troy and Bobbie laughed without compassion. They laughed again a few minutes later when Jeff looked in the creel and told Troy he was impressed with his fishing ability.

"What did I say?" he asked after the laughter died down.

"Tell him, Bobbie," Troy prompted her.

Strangely enough, Bobbie was a little embarrassed. When she didn't say anything, Jeff sat down beside her and took the pole from her hands.

"You really should have brought Gil along. He's the best fisherman in the family. But then I'm not sure he could compete with you, Bobbie, since I'm sure you must be the one who caught most of those fish."

Thinking that Jeff never took long to catch on, Bobbie didn't look at him. She was still angry with herself for the way her face heated up, and knowing that he was staring at her profile just caused her face to flush all over again.

"I'll take these back," Troy said after a moment. "When you catch more you can string them." Bobbie and Jeff were silent as they listened to the sound of Troy's footsteps. Bobbie glanced over at Jeff to find him still staring at her. She returned the look and wondered what he was thinking. She didn't wait long to find out.

thirty-five

"You were embarrassed in front of me just now. I want to know why." Jeff's voice was undemanding, but Bobbie knew he would sit right where he was until he had an answer.

"Come on, Bobbie," he coaxed after a moment. "There isn't anything you can't tell me."

"It's just my pride, Jeff," she admitted quietly.

"I don't understand."

Bobbie ran a self-conscious hand through her hair, wishing she had taken a comb to it. "It doesn't matter that our friendship isn't a romantic one, Jeff; no girl likes to be caught with her hair uncombed, wearing denim pants, and catching fish so well that she's mistaken for a man." Bobbie shrugged apologetically. "Like I said, Jeff, it's just my pride."

Jeff stared at her incredulously. *Was she serious?* It took him a moment to see that she was. "I don't think there's anything you could do, Bobbie," Jeff replied softly, "that would cause you to be mistaken for a man."

It was Bobbie's turn to stare. Jeff returned her scrutiny,

their eyes meeting with questions and a hesitancy that had never been present in their relationship before.

Bobbie watched as Jeff's eyes dropped to her mouth, and her throat went dry. With his free hand he reached out to touch the corner of her mouth with a single finger, just brushing it with a single caress. He shook his head slowly as he spoke in a whisper.

"Maybe the most adorable thing in Santa Rosa, but definitely *not* a man."

Bobbie didn't know what to say. She turned her head back to the water and Jeff did the same.

"I don't seem to be doing very well with this pole. Maybe I'd better give it back to you."

Bobbie took the offer for what it was, a chance to return the conversation to comfortable ground. They fished for another 20 minutes and then headed back to camp for breakfast with three more fish.

Once again Jeff believed the rest of the weekend would be awkward, but all was fine. The day passed in friendship and laughter and both Jeff and Bobbie were relieved that the uncomfortable moment on the creek bank had passed without harm.

As the sun sank lower in the afternoon sky, Bobbie told Marcail to gather her things for their Saturday night bath. Jake accompanied the girls and sat well out of sight with his gun, but close enough to assist if they should call.

He had brought his Bible along, but the laughter and splashes he heard made him put his head back against the rock where he had sat down, and smile. Bobbie was always so much fun, he mused. Marcail must have thought so too, since her laughter seemed to be nonstop.

Not until this weekend did Jake notice the way Bobbie and Jeff treated each other. Maryanne had mentioned her observations to him, but he thought little of it. Jake had the distinct impression that something wasn't quite right when they returned from fishing, but the rest of the day went on in such a normal fashion that Jake doubted his own thoughts.

In fact, he put the whole thing out of his mind until he came back with the girls. He had never given any thought to it before, but a woman with wet hair needed to have privacy. At least Jake began to think so as he noticed Jeff watching Bobbie attentively.

Since Bobbie's hair was short and curly she didn't do much to it until it was dry, and then all she did was fluff the waves up to make them a little fuller. With her hair in close damp curls all around her head, she looked like she had just come from her bath, which she had, and that seemed very personal to Jake.

He watched his daughter and Jeff closely for a time, but there was nothing intimate about their actions. They shared light banter and their legs were nearly touching as Marcail sat in Jeff's lap so Bobbie could brush her hair.

Jake could make no sense of it. He and Maryanne hadn't acted that way until after they were married. Jake entertained thoughts of speaking to Jeff, but prayed instead. The Lord gave him an unexpected peace and he let the matter drop in his mind.

Bobbie prayed for just such a peace several hours later. Supper was over and it was quite dark. Everyone was in his bedroll. Marcail was sound asleep beside her, but slumber simply would not come for Bobbie. Replaying the scene from the creek again and again in her mind, the words of a friend from church spoken weeks before haunted her.

"Bobbie, if you're not going to marry Jeffrey Taylor, let him go so one of us can."

Bobbie had laughed and made some remark that made the whole group of girls roar, but Bobbie didn't feel like laughing now. Earlier in the afternoon Bobbie and Jeff had talked about his date with Sylvia.

"We had fun," Jeff had told her. "Sylvia has changed lately, and we talked about things we've never discussed before. We have another date Monday night."

Bobbie had been glad for him. She knew from Jeff's own admission how badly he felt about not seeing her, but they both had known it was for the best. The only person who hadn't known was Sylvia. Jeff and Bobbie had both prayed she would come to a peace about that. Now it seemed Sylvia had.

It also seemed that Jeff and Sylvia were going to be seeing each other again, and in Bobbie's mind that could only mean matrimony. But if that were the case, then why had Jeff talked to her and touched her as though she were someone special? Not just special, but *special*?

This and many other questions kept Bobbie awake far into the night. The next morning she was so sleepy that she figured it must have been the wee morning hours before sleep finally claimed her.

She was by nature a morning person, but today all she did for the first half-hour was sit and stare into her coffee cup. She heard the teasing remarks from her family and Jeff, but all she could do was smile.

"Are you all right?" The question came from her father after Troy and Jeff went to the creek to clean up.

"Just tired."

"I heard you tossing in the wagon for quite awhile."

"I hope I didn't keep you awake."

"No. You want to talk?"

Bobbie's voice dropped as she answered. "Not when we might be interrupted, but thanks."

Jake followed his daughter's gaze and they both watched Marcail approach. She was having the time of her young life.

"Do we really have to go back today, Bobbie?" were the first words from her mouth.

"I'm afraid so, Marcail." Jake answered for Bobbie, who was still pretty fuzzy around the edges.

"I take it you've had fun," Bobbie finally said.

Marcail didn't answer, but smiled at Bobbie and Jake with the shy smile which came over her face when she was at a loss for words.

Troy and Jeff made a tremendous amount of noise coming back into camp. Troy's hair was completely wet and both men were laughing. When Troy stopped chuckling he explained that Jeff had bumped him as he knelt on the bank, and he had gone face-first into the water. His hands had stopped the rest of his body from going in, but the whole incident had been such a surprise that he had been sure he was about to drown.

Jeff apologized twice during a breakfast of pancakes, but he was laughing too hard to be taken seriously. After the dishes were done the campers sat on the logs while Jake read from the Scriptures.

"This is James, chapter one, verses two through six. 'My brethren, count it all joy when ye fall into diverse temptations, knowing this, that the trying of your faith worketh patience. But let patience have her perfect work, that ye may be perfect and entire, wanting nothing. If any of you lack wisdom, let him ask of God, who giveth to all men liberally and upbraideth not, and it shall be given him. But let him ask in faith, nothing wavering. For he that wavereth is like a wave of the sea driven with the wind and tossed.'"

They had a time of prayer after the Bible was closed, with Jake opening and Troy closing. Jeff now understood what Bobbie meant when she said they had their own service when they slept too late at home, and why she said she always enjoyed it.

With plans to be back home for lunch, they began to break camp a short time later. Jeff, Bobbie, and Marcail were once again in the back, and Bobbie asked the youngest camper how she enjoyed the weekend.

"When can we come again?"

Jeff laughed. "I guess that answers your question."

"Did you have fun, Jeff?" Marcail wanted to know.

"Oh yes," Jeff said with conviction. "Everything was great. It was also enlightening, and that was something I hadn't planned on."

Jeff said these last words as if he were alone, and even though neither Bobbie nor Marcail questioned him, Bobbie thought about it all the way home.

thirty-six

Bobbie was getting ready to go to lunch on Monday when Carla Johnson walked into the shipping office.

"Hi, Carla."

"Hi, Bobbie, are you by any chance free for lunch?"

"I was just getting ready to leave. Let me check with Bill to see if he's ready to let me go."

Carla waited while Bobbie knocked on Bill's door and was given permission to leave.

"Where shall we go?" Bobbie wanted to know.

"To the hotel."

"The hotel? What's the occasion?"

Carla waited until they were a few steps up the street. "The occasion is that Troy came over last night and told me he wants to be married right away. When I asked how come the change of heart, he said it was because of something you said."

Bobbie stopped in her tracks and stared at Carla. The next instant they were hugging and Bobbie was fighting tears. Once at the hotel Carla found them a table and they talked nonstop for the next hour.

"Can you please tell me what you said to Troy this weekend?"

Bobbie shrugged. "It wasn't much. I asked him if you two were going to be married and when he said yes, I asked what he was waiting for. To put it simply, I criticized him for his reasons. I could see it made him think."

Carla sighed. "Thanks, Bobbie. I've wanted to bring up the subject of my working for a long time, but I felt that might be pushing him. Until last night, I wasn't *really* sure he wanted to marry me because he always used that reason. I just never thought it had any validity."

"So what are your plans now?"

"First of all, your parents are coming to supper tomorrow night, and the six of us—that includes my folks—are going to talk. Will you feel bad, Bobbie, because you're not there?"

"Just awful," Bobbie said with a smile. "I'll pout all evening. Now tell me more!"

"We'd like to be married right away, say in a month, with just a quiet ceremony. Then, after we've been away for a few days on a honeymoon trip, we'd like to come home, get settled in our house, and have a reception with the church family."

"I think that sounds wonderful! Where will you live?"

"That's one of the items we need to discuss with our folks. With Troy working on this side of town, it would be nice to find a place close by."

Lunch had been served to the ladies, but they had barely taken notice. Bobbie commented that she better eat or she would go back to work hungry. Carla continued to tell her future sister-in-law of her plans, and long before they were done Bobbie had to go back the shipping office, wishing as she did that she had time to find Troy and hug him.

Bobbie was almost as dreamy as Carla had been at lunch when she went back to work. But preoccupied as she was, she did not fail to notice how distracted Jeff seemed. He was polite, but it was clear that something weighed on his mind.

Bobbie was not given an opportunity to question him, but when Sylvia came in at closing time Jeff instantly perked up. Bobbie was relieved to witness such a scene, since it gave her peace of mind over his odd behavior. Jeff excused himself for a moment to finish some business.

"'Hello, Bobbie," Sylvia greeted her quietly from where she waited by the door. Bobbie finally recalled Jeff saying he had a date with Sylvia.

"Hi, Sylvia. Come over, sit down."

Sylvia took one of the chairs by the desk, and even though Bobbie had things to do, she set her pencil aside and smiled at the stunning blonde.

"How was your weekend?" Sylvia wanted to know.

"It was great. The weather was perfect and I know that Marcail had the time of her life. How were things here in town?"

"Pretty quiet, I think, although church was full." Sylvia hesitated a moment and then rushed on. "Bobbie, there's something I need to say to you."

Bobbie smiled expectantly and waited.

"I've never apologized to you for the way I acted at the lagoon, but I'm sorry. I'm also sorry that it's taken me this long to tell you." Sylvia's face was flushed and Bobbie realized how difficult it must have been for Sylvia to hold that in all these years.

"Thank you, Sylvia," Bobbie said simply and gave Sylvia a smile of such serenity that her fears of rejection drained away in an instant.

The women talked until Jeff returned. Sylvia told Bobbie about Pastor's sermon and Bobbie shared with Sylvia about her niece and nephew. Their chatter was random, and how they chose those subjects was not clear. What *was* clear was there was no more constraint between them. They laughed and talked in a normal way, with none of the awkwardness that had been the hallmark of their previous conversations.

When Jeff finally came from the office to claim Sylvia, Bobbie bid her goodbye, feeling like she had a new friend. On the other hand, her old friend Jeff was still perplexed about something. She had seen it in his face when he had said goodbye to her. Bobbie began praying as soon as she went back to her work that God would open a door for them to talk.

Bobbie would have been surprised to know that Sylvia was praying for that very thing as she sat with Jeff in the hotel. Jeff was absorbed in some private distraction, and Sylvia, although not angry, was quite determined to find out if she was the cause.

"How was work?"

"Fine." Jeff told her.

"And your weekend?"

"Great," Jeff said softly, and warning bells went off in Sylvia's mind.

"You didn't say that very enthusiastically."

"Didn't I?" Jeff was truly surprised. He then went on to describe every detail of the camping experience, and Sylvia couldn't help but wonder if Jeff knew how his eyes softened just a bit whenever he mentioned Bobbie's name. In fact he made it sound like an endearment.

Their supper together was relaxed, but when Jeff saw Sylvia home she was quiet. Jeff, who was equally silent, didn't seem to notice. Once at the house Jeff suddenly seemed to realize how preoccupied he had been.

"I'm sorry, Sylvia, I don't seem to be very good company tonight."

"It's not happening for you, is it, Jeff?"

It took him a moment to understand Sylvia as she gazed at him with her heart in her eyes. A look of profound remorse passed over Jeff's features and Sylvia did her best to smile.

"It's all right, Jeff. You can't force something you don't feel."

"I do care for you, Sylvia."

"I know you do," she said with soft regret. "I also know that there's someone who already holds your heart, and I wonder when you're going to open your eyes and see that."

Without giving Jeff a chance to speak, Sylvia went up on tiptoes to kiss his cheek.

"Goodbye, Jeff."

Jeff didn't move or reply even after Sylvia went into her sister's house and shut the door. He stood motionless for the space of a few heartbeats.

"My eyes are open, Sylvia." Jeff's voice was hushed as he walked away from the house. "But hers aren't, and I don't know what to do about that."

❑❑❑

Sylvia leaned against the closed door and shut her eyes tightly. 'It's time for me to go home.'

"Sylvia, is that you already?"

"It's me."

"How was your date?" Sandra asked kindly as Sylvia joined her in the empty living room.

"It was fine." Sylvia's voice was quiet. "But I won't be seeing Jeff again."

Sandra was silent as she digested this new information. A few months ago she would have scathingly asked what Sylvia had done this time to drive Jeff away. But Sylvia's sudden maturity made this question unnecessary.

"Are you all right?" the older woman finally asked.

"I will be. I think I should tell you now that I've decided to go home in a few weeks."

"So soon?" The question alone spoke volumes as to the changes Sandra and Carl had seen in Sylvia since she returned from Aunt Velvet's.

Sylvia could only nod and the women shared an embrace. It had been a long time coming, but Sylvia Weber was finally growing up.

thirty-seven

The next four weeks were taken up with preparations for Troy's wedding and his moving into the small house that Kaitlin and Marcail had lived in when they first arrived in Santa Rosa. Carla had been ecstatic to find that it was free to rent just two weeks before the date. The church reception was not planned until three weeks after the wedding, so Maryanne and Mrs. Johnson dug into their attics and trunks to find needed household goods.

It was a rather ragtag collection of bedding and kitchen supplies when it was put together, but Troy and Carla only had eyes for each other.

With only the Johnsons, Bradfords, and Pastor Keller in attendance, the ceremony was as simple and quiet as the young couple hoped it would be. The newlyweds were headed a few hours north for their honeymoon.

Troy's absence from the house made it feel empty. Bobbie's heart seemed a little empty too, and even though the void was not directly related to Troy, it did have something to do with seeing him and Carla stand before Pastor Keller and become husband and wife. Bobbie coveted the title of wife.

Unbidden, Jeff's face came to mind, and Bobbie shook her head to dispel the vision. Jeff belonged to Sylvia. He hadn't talked much about his dates with her lately, but Bobbie suspected they were becoming quite serious with the way Jeff seemed to be putting more and more space between himself and Bobbie.

Bobbie longed to talk with him, but knew she couldn't be close friends with a married man, and that it would be easier in the long run to start thinking of Jeff in that light right now.

What Bobbie didn't expect was that her feelings would be stronger than she was, and that the reception, held at one of the large homes where Maryanne worked, would end in humiliation for Bobbie.

❑❑❑

"I can't believe Mrs. Walcott let us use her home and garden." It was the fifth time Maryanne had made such a statement, and as before, Jake smiled to himself and kept quiet.

"Do we have everything? Where's Bobbie? What time is it?" Jake was not given a chance to answer any of these questions, and actually he didn't even try.

Maryanne was quiet on the way to Walcotts', but as soon as they arrived she began giving orders like a woman possessed. Jake listened to her for a few minutes before stepping in.

"Mary," he said softly, "everything is going to be fine, and if you don't stop telling Bobbie to be in four places at once, she's going to run away."

Stopped short over her husband's words, Maryanne apologized to her daughter and prayed for calm. Things were a little smoother from that point on, and when the guests began to arrive, everything was in place.

The Walcott mansion was a tall, broad, two-story house with a backyard garden which was the envy of Santa Rosa residents. The kitchen and summer porch at the rear of the house made a garden reception a dream.

Tables and chairs were scattered all over the lush grass and faced the long tables set up outside the kitchen door for the finger foods, cakes, and fruit drinks. Guests could roam about at will or sit next to the flowerbeds, whose riotous colors only enhanced the occasion for which the church family was gathered.

Carla was radiant and Troy's smile nearly stretched off his face as he stood beside his wife. The Johnsons mingled with Jake and Maryanne while Bobbie ran back and forth from the kitchen to the beautiful garden all afternoon.

By the time the guests began to leave, the gift table was laden and the food tables were nearly bare. Cleanup was a momentous task and Bobbie was again involved. She had just pushed a wheeled cart into a rather secluded dining room where Mrs. Walcott kept her large platters, in the bottom drawer of a buffet, when she felt her glasses fall from her face.

Quickly reacting this time, she grasped both pieces as they slid down her front. She had been standing for at least five minutes trying to put them together on her own when she heard someone enter the room.

"Your mother told me I might find you in here."

"Oh, hi, Jeff. She now knew his voice so well. My glasses came apart. I know how to fix them when they break like this, but I just can't get it."

"Here, let me have a go."

Bobbie surrendered the glasses to his capable hands, and as always drew very close to watch him work. Jeff was able to snap them back together, and Bobbie waited while he wiped the lenses before placing them gently back on her face.

He leaned close as he always did when helping her with her spectacles, and even after the lenses were in place he stayed bent over her, their noses nearly touching.

Jeff smiled as Bobbie's eyes focused on him. Bobbie smiled back, thinking how much she had missed being close to him. When Jeff did not immediately move away, Bobbie acted without thought. She put one hand, almost a caress, against the side of Jeff's face and pressed her lips to his.

As though completely forgetting that she had no right to do such a thing, Bobbie did not immediately check herself and step away, making the moment she *did* realize she was actually kissing Jeff the most embarrassing thing to ever happen to her.

Jeff's gaze was very tender as Bobbie broke the kiss and took a hasty step backward, but she didn't notice. With one hand to her throat, she began to stutter.

"Jeff, I'm s-sorry. I c-can't think what c-came over m-me."

"Bobbie, honey—"

"No, Jeff, don't say anything. I'm just so sorry." Bobbie turned away from him then, and when she looked back, there were tears in her eyes. "Sylvia will never forgive me," she whispered.

"Bobbie, please—"

Jeff stopped and didn't follow her when she rushed past him and out of the room. He found himself looking around and thanking God that the room had provided privacy. The last thing they had needed was witnesses. Jeff exited the room determined to find her and clear things up, but she was nowhere to be found.

He went to her house that evening just before supper, but Jake told him that Bobbie had gone to bed exhausted. Jeff determined to pin her down the next day at church, but she avoided him nicely, and when he went to her house on Sunday afternoon, Maryanne said she was at her sister's.

Feeling frustrated, Jeff left telling himself there was always tomorrow. And unless Bobbie had quit her job when he wasn't looking, she would have to face him at the office in the morning.

thirty-eight

Bobbie's Sunday was miserable as she walked over half of Santa Rosa. Never had she handled anything so badly as her mistake with Jeff. Running from him was the worst thing she could do, but the blood drained from her face every time she thought of facing him with an apology, or working with him on a daily basis.

It was her thought life that had gotten her into trouble, of that she was positive. Very recently she had imagined herself kissing Jeff on more than one occasion, and when he had bent so close, Sylvia had been the farthest person from her mind. She hadn't even tried to stop herself.

Again Bobbie found herself having to confess how much she had enjoyed it. If only he hadn't fallen for Sylvia. Jeff was sure to marry Sylvia. *If only,* Bobbie thought, and then stopped herself. She would never keep going if her life was a series of *if only's.*

There was no choice about her job—she would have to quit, of course. Fear of running into Jeff kept her from going to see Mr. Taylor that very afternoon. Bobbie tried to push away the pain that returned again and again on her walk.

Maryanne had not lied to Jeff. Before going on a long walk to think and pray, Bobbie had gone to see her sister for a brief visit. In no less pain when she finally returned home, Bobbie had at least told God all she felt, and she knew what must be done.

Her parents had questioned her about being gone so long, but in fear of starting tears that would never stop, Bobbie had not answered. Neither Jake nor Maryanne had pushed the point, but they watched with concern as Bobbie played with her supper and ate no breakfast the following morning.

"Bobbie," Maryanne stopped her daughter as she was headed out the door for work. "If you're not feeling well, you can stay home."

"I know, Mom, and I know you're wondering what's going on, but I just can't talk about it right now. I hope when I get home tonight I'll be able to explain everything."

Maryanne, feeling she had no choice but to accept her grown daughter's answer, was very concerned. "I'll be praying for you, Bobbie."

Those words were nearly her undoing. How easy it would be to run to the protective arms of her parents! And then Bobbie stopped short. She was done running a long time ago. She squared her shoulders with renewed purpose.

"Thanks, Mom, I appreciate that." Kissing her mother's cheek, Bobbie headed toward the door and called over her shoulder, "I'll see you tonight."

thirty-nine

"You sure know how to avoid a man."

Bobbie started at the sound of Jeff's voice and felt her face flush. Overcome with regret, she didn't say anything for a few moments. A wonderful friendship had been ruined. They would never be comfortable with each other again, and it was all her fault.

That Jeff was extremely glad to see her was totally lost on Bobbie. Drowning in her own hurt, she failed to notice how Jeff's eyes sparkled with tenderness and warmth.

"Bobbie—"

"Please, Jeff, just let me say how—"

"Hello, Jeff; hello, Bobbie." Bobbie was interrupted by May's sudden entrance to the shipping office. She held Marcail's hand, and Bobbie, without delay, forgot her own problems at the sight of the white-faced little girl.

"It seems that Kaitlin chose today to have her baby, and I told Marcail it would be a good idea if she came here for a few hours."

"That's a great idea. Come over and have a chair, Marc." The words were spoken by Jeff, and with his hand on the little girl's shoulder, she was escorted up to Bobbie's desk.

May left quietly and a few minutes later Bill entered the office. Bobbie was speaking with Marcail and didn't hear the exchange between father and son, but when Bill went into his office Jeff suggested that Bobbie and Marcail take a ride with him.

Once in the wagon, Jeff and Bobbie's eyes met over the top of Marcail's head and it was with mutual, unspoken understanding that they decided to put their discussion off and concentrate on their young charge.

Marcail had said little, and as Jeff headed the wagon in the direction of the lagoon, Bobbie asked God to give her the words to comfort and help Marcail.

❑❑❑

Kaitlin spat a sentence at Rigg in furious Hawaiian. It was the second time she had said it to him, and for the first time he was glad he couldn't speak the language.

"I can't push anymore, Rigg, I just can't do it," Kate panted after the last hard contraction.

Rigg mopped her brow and kissed her cheek. No one had ever told him it would be like this. No one had ever mentioned that his wife would be in agony for hours and he would be powerless to help.

Rigg had not previously known the meaning of the word "frustration" until Doctor Grade had come, checked on Kaitlin, and left, telling them it would probably be some hours yet. He had told them where he could be found and his manner had been kind, but Rigg, unsatisfied, had followed him to the door.

"Isn't there anything you can do for her?"

"I'm afraid not, Rigg. First babies take time."

Rigg found out in a hurry that those words had been an understatement. It felt to him as though Kate had been in labor for days, and he wasn't even the one in pain.

"Oh no," Kate gasped as another contraction began. Rigg looked at his mother on the other side of the bed to see if she was as worried as he was, but the smile she gave him was one of serene acceptance.

Illumination flooded Rigg's heart as he realized that his mother had gone through this exact process to have him. Kate needed him right now, so there was no time for talk, but when this was all over, and Rigg prayed it would be soon, he told himself he was going to thank Mabel Riggs Taylor for giving him life.

❑❑❑

"You were really on a date here?" Marcail asked in childish wonder. "What did you do?"

"Well," Bobbie explained, "the other kids were here as well, and we had a picnic lunch under the trees. Then we sat around and talked. The whole church came later to go boating."

"Can we go boating?"

"Not today, but I think we might be able to arrange something later on," Jeff had answered from the place where he was sitting with his back against a tree. He was amazed at the relaxed way Bobbie talked about the day at the lagoon, without giving any hint of the disastrous events that followed.

He was also amazed how strong his feelings were for her. They were both doing a good job of pretending there was nothing they needed to discuss. Jeff was sure Marcail didn't suspect a thing. She was growing visibly more relaxed by the second, and that fact was directly related to Bobbie's sensitive care of her.

"I think it might be getting close to lunch. Shall we go back to my house to eat?"

"I don't know, Bobbie. Maybe I should go and check on Katie."

"I think it would be best if we didn't go over there right now."

"Why, Bobbie? Why did May take me away? What are they doing to Katie that they don't want me to know?"

Bobbie's arms went around the little girl. "They're not *doing* anything to her Marcail, but it's hard work having a baby, and it's not the best idea to have a lot of people around."

"But there *were* a lot of people around, even Dr. Grade."

"Marc," Bobbie said softly, "Dr. Grade is there to help Katie. He's there to take care of her."

Marcail was certain she was going to return home and have Rigg tell her that Kate was dying, but she didn't mention any of this to Bobbie.

"The people at the house are there for a reason. And even though I'm sure Katie wishes you could be nearby, she also sees that it would be easier if you were elsewhere. It would be the same as if you wanted to go to work at the livery with Sean. He'd like to have your company, but you couldn't really help him with his job, and it would be easier for him if you weren't there.

"Having a baby is work. If Kate is worried about you, then she won't be able to work as well as she needs to."

Some of the tension that had returned to Marcail's face drained away, and they got in the wagon to head for the Bradfords. Jeff was careful not to look in the direction of his brother's place as they rode through town, but he couldn't help but wonder if his sister-in-law was all right. He prayed for all concerned and tried to turn his mind back to the situation at hand.

❑❑❑

Sean came out of his chair in the kitchen as though someone had jerked him up on a string. His sister had just let out a bloodcurdling scream, and he waited, his breath held, for some noise to issue from the bedroom.

Black spots dotted his vision a moment later when he heard a baby cry. He sat back down with a thud, hoping he wouldn't faint. A baby! His sister had had a baby!

forty

Sean watched May emerge from the bedroom, wiping her eyes.

"A girl, a big beautiful girl."

Her words started the young man's own tears. Kate had confided in him one day that most men wanted boys, but that Rigg had wanted a daughter. She had said it was her deepest desire to give him that wish.

"Is Kate all right?" Sean asked hesitantly over the lump in his throat.

"She's fine. Just give them a few minutes and you can go in."

It was less than two minutes before the door was thrown open and Rigg appeared, disheveled but beaming.

"Sean! Get in here and see your niece! Where's Marc?"

"I'll go and find her," May said with more calm than she felt. It was an exhilarating experience to see your first grandchild enter the world, and she was feeling a bit light-headed about it.

Rigg gave his mother an enormous hug before reaching for his brother-in-law. Sean noticed tears in the big man's eyes and fought the return of his own as he stepped softly into the bedroom. He focused on his sister and she gave him a tired smile.

Sean felt his own fatigue when he saw that smile. He hadn't realized how tense he had been, but Kate was all right, he could see that. Everything was going to be fine because Kaitlin was all right.

"Aren't you going to look at her?"

"Oh, sorry, Kate," Sean nearly stuttered. He had been so worried about Kate that he forgot about the new little life his sister held in the curve of her arm.

Sean couldn't stop the frown that crossed his face at the first sight of his niece, and Kate chuckled softly.

"She's a funny-looking little thing, isn't she, Sean?"

"Well—" Sean wanted to disagree, but couldn't.

The baby was red and wrinkly and her face looked as if some fierce battle was going on inside of her. Her eyes opened as Sean watched, and she waved one tiny red fist in the air. Sean's heart melted.

"What's her name?" he asked when he could find his voice again.

"We thought we'd let Marcail decide," Rigg said from his place on the opposite side of the bed.

"That's a good idea," Sean said with conviction. He hadn't seen much of his family over the summer, but he knew that Kate's pregnancy had been very hard on his little sister. Marcail's naming the baby was probably just what she needed to help her adjust to the changes that would certainly enter their home in the next few months.

❑ ❑ ❑

"There will be certain changes."

"What kind of changes?"

"Good ones," Bobbie answered. "You can be a tremendous help to Kaitlin with the baby. In fact the baby will probably think of you as a second mother, since you live in the same house."

Marcail was so pleased with Bobbie's words that she was actually able to eat some lunch. She was just finishing when May knocked on the door.

"I thought I might find you here," May said as she entered the room. "You have a perfect little niece." May gave Marcail a hug after making her announcement, or she might have noticed the worried look that had suddenly captured the little girl's features.

Why doesn't anyone say how Kate is doing? The question tormented Marcail all the way home, but she kept her thoughts to herself and tried not to vomit. Rigg greeted her at the door with a big smile and Marcail took heart. He wouldn't look like that if Kate was in heaven with Mother, would he?

More chance for speculation was cut short when Rigg led her quietly into the bedroom. She told herself not to be sick when she saw Kate's closed eyes, but she didn't know how long she would be able to hold herself together. Marcail stood stock-still about two feet from what she was sure was Kate's dead body and wished she hadn't eaten lunch.

Rigg watched his sister-in-law in silence. Her hands were clenched so tightly that her knuckles were white. Marcail's eyes were fixed on Kate's sleeping face and Rigg wondered if she might faint. She hadn't been anywhere near the basket that held his daughter, and he wished with all his heart he knew what she was thinking.

A few more seconds passed and Kaitlin opened her eyes. Rigg nearly reached for Marcail, since she seemed to go very limp. Kaitlin smiled at her little sister and that was Marcail's undoing. Rivers of silent tears poured down her cheeks and she choked when she tried to speak.

"I thought," Marcail coughed and then took a deep breath, "I thought you were dead."

"Oh Marcail!" Kate was equally choked up as she leaned toward her sister. Marcail was too far from the bed for Kate to reach her, and blinded by her tears, she didn't notice her sister's outstretched arm, so Rigg propelled her forward with a gentle hand. He took a chair by the bed and wiped the tears from his own eyes over Marcail's reaction.

It hadn't occurred to anyone that she might think her sister was dying. Of course it was blindness on their part, because they all knew how tense Marcail became whenever a doctor was called onto the scene. He realized now, as he took a moment to think, that she had almost been sick as she stood and watched Kate.

"Am I hurting you, Katie?"

"No."

Marcail had climbed right onto the bed with her sister and wrapped her arms around her neck. Kate held her protectively and her small body trembled from head to foot. Rigg had just placed a blanket over the top of her when she went very stiff. Marcail half-sat so she could look into her sister's face.

"You had a baby."

"That's right, I did." Kaitlin smiled. She had wondered when Marcail was going to ask.

"Where is she?"

"In the basket right over there."

Marcail left the bed gently and found Rigg smiling at her. She put her hand to her mouth and whispered. "I forgot about the baby for a minute."

"That's all right," Rigg whispered back.

Husband and wife watched as she made her way across the room. "Oh my," was all they heard for some moments.

"What's her name?" Marcail asked without ever taking her eyes from the sleeping infant.

"We were hoping *you* would tell *us*," Rigg answered softly.

Marcail finally turned and looked at Rigg and then her sister. Kate nodded encouragingly and Marcail's little mouth dropped open in surprise.

"You want *me* to name her?"

No one answered Marcail, but Rigg motioned her to the chair he had just vacated and scooped his tiny daughter into his hands. As Kate looked on, Rigg placed her in Marcail's arms.

"You did everything you could to make Kate's pregnancy easier," Rigg said as he helped Marcail hold the baby in the right position. "In fact I think you would have carried the baby yourself if you could have. So we want you to name your niece because we know how much you love her."

Marcail looked with wonder at the tiny person in her arms. She was just perfect. She held her a little closer in one arm and reached with her free hand to the silky thatch of black hair that covered the very top of the baby's head and hung in uneven wisps down her forehead. She fingered the hair for just a moment before turning a smiling face to the adults in the room.

"Gretchen." Marcail said softly. "How do you like Gretchen Riggs after Rigg's grandmother?"

"It's perfect."

"I love it."

"Why, we never would have thought of it!"

Rigg and Kate were so pleased over the name that their words stumbled over the top of one another. But the ten-year-old aunt holding the baby didn't notice. Her eyes were riveted on the tiny niece cuddled in her arms.

Rigg and Kate beamed as they watched the two in the chair. Rigg leaned and kissed Kate softly on the mouth.

"I believe she's feeling a little bit of what I felt when I first laid eyes on you," Rigg said softly to his wife.

"And what was that exactly?"

"Nothing short of love at first sight." They kissed again and neither one heard Marcail whispering to the baby.

"I love you, Gretchen Riggs. I love you like you were my very own."

forty-one

Bobbie was very pleased to be heading home for the day. She was emotionally and physically spent. It had seemed to take forever for Marcail to emerge from Rigg and Kaitlin's bedroom. Bobbie had stayed in the living room with May, Jeff, and Sean. She found the pretense of acting as though everything was fine more difficult every second.

It had been over a half-hour before she had been able to see the baby and excuse herself. May drove her back to the shipping office so she could tell Bill and Gilbert the news. Bobbie had worked the rest of the day as well as locked up that evening.

She had missed out on seeing Paige and Wesley when they were infants, and Bobbie's throat had been so tight at her first view of Gretchen that she could barely swallow.

Once home, she halfway hoped that Jeff would come by so she could apologize to him, but she ate her supper and went to bed without seeing him.

Two hours after Bobbie blew out her lamp she was still

awake. The moon was full, so after slipping her spectacles back onto her nose, she found her robe and went to the kitchen. She had lit the lamp and was preparing a snack when her mother joined her.

"Did I wake you?"

"Yes, but that's all right."

The women worked on cups of tea and sandwiches in silence. When they did begin to speak it was about small things—dress material that Maryanne had seen, how nice the gifts at the reception had been, and how quickly the summer had gone. When Bobbie had finished her sandwich and half of her tea she confided to her mother about what happened in the dining room at the Walcotts'.

"I think I'm in love with him, Mom, but that doesn't give me the right to kiss him. I mean, he and Sylvia are seeing each other and I think they might get married. I told myself I would never run again, but I've got to tell Bill I'll be looking for work somewhere else in town."

Maryanne was quiet. She was praying for words of comfort and Bobbie began to think she was upset.

"You're disappointed in me, aren't you?"

"Oh, Bob, no! I don't know where you got such an idea. I'm sitting here praying for you. I don't think you should have kissed Jeff, but *everyone* makes mistakes."

Maryanne's voice lowered with intensity. "You do understand that, don't you, Bobbie? Just confess this and go on, even if you have to find work elsewhere. Apologize to Jeff and then to the Lord. Ask Him to take you on from here."

Bobbie nodded in agreement. She was coming to the same conclusion, but she felt so badly about everything that she wasn't even sure how to pray most of the time.

"It's too bad in some ways," Maryanne continued. "You couldn't ask for a nicer boss. After you'd gone upstairs this evening, he dropped by to tell you to take the morning off."

"You're right; Mr. Taylor is wonderful. And I'm going to need the morning off after staying up all night."

"My Bible is in the bedroom, Bobbie, and that's where I need to be. But tomorrow, before you go to work to talk to Jeff, read Romans eight, 26 and 27. Those are verses about prayer, and I suspect you need them right now."

Maryanne hugged Bobbie and headed up the stairs. Bobbie followed soon afterward, and this time, with a prayer in her heart for the coming events of the day, she fell asleep quickly.

❑❑❑

"I'm glad you were here, Jeff, since my decision to leave was so sudden and I thought I would have to miss you."

"I'm glad too, Sylvia, and I'll be praying that you have a safe trip."

"Thanks, Jeff."

"Well, I guess this is goodbye. I don't plan to be back in Santa Posa anytime soon. You've been a true friend, Jeff, and I'll never forget you."

Jeff and Sylvia embraced in a final goodbye as Sandra came out of the stage office. Jeff stepped away to give the sisters some privacy. He stayed on the platform until the stage pulled away, waving when Sylvia's head appeared in the window.

Jeff returned to the office intent on asking his father

when Bobbie would be in, but Bill sent him on an errand. 'It was just as well,' he thought as he left. The office was no place for the showdown he was planning.

❑❑❑

"Likewise the Spirit also helpeth our infirmities; for we know not what we should pray for as we ought, but the Spirit itself maketh intercession for us with groanings which can not be uttered. And he that searcheth the hearts knoweth what is the mind of the Spirit, because he maketh intercession for the saints according to the will of God."

Bobbie prayed long and hard over the words she had just read. They were exactly what she needed. She felt with all her heart that God wanted her to trust Him.

'Thank You for these verses, Father, and for Your mightiness and power and for Your faithfulness. You know my heart and how much I want to make things right. Please give me the words with Jeff and Mr. Taylor today. I want to run from this, God, but I know I can't. Help me to trust You. Please give me the needed strength and wisdom.'

Bobbie did not end the prayer but continued to petition God silently all the way to work. She found Bill in his office and he greeted her warmly. Talking proudly about his new granddaughter for several minutes, he finally noticed that his employee had something on her mind.

"Did you need something, Bobbie?"

"Yes, actually I do. I've decided to take a few weeks off just as soon as you can spare me, and then I'm going to look for work someplace else in town." Bill opened his mouth to object, but Bobbie rushed on.

"It has nothing to do with you or the work here at the office, and I want to thank you for all you've done."

"Bobbie," Bill finally cut in, looking a little thunderstruck, "is there something I can do? I mean, your work here is excellent and if there's anything I can say to change your mind, just—"

"No, but thank you." Bobbie stood, telling Bill that her mind was made up.

"Is Jeff around?" Bobbie asked with her hand on the door handle.

"No, I asked him to run uptown."

Bobbie nodded. "I guess I better get to work."

Bobbie left the inner office still praying, and she congratulated herself over not bursting into tears. She had only been at her desk a few minutes when Bill came out and asked her to take something to Rigg.

Bobbie complied, but she was disappointed since she wanted to see Jeff right away. The Lord reminded her then to trust Him, and Bobbie stopped herself from scanning the street in hopes of spotting him.

❑❑❑

"I'm telling you, Dad, she won't be quitting."

"Jeff," Bill said with extreme patience, "she was just in here and told me herself."

"You're repeating yourself, Dad. I'm telling you that as soon as she comes back, I'll talk with her and get this whole thing worked out."

"So you're the reason she wants to quit?" Gilbert commented softly.

"Not exactly, but my presence is making her uncomfortable. I'm sure she plans on apologizing to me and then walking away. What she doesn't know is that I'm not about to let her do that."

Bill and Gilbert were left staring at each other in confusion as Jeff walked out of the room.

forty-two

Jeff was next door when Bobbie came back. She went straight to her desk to work, wondering yet again when she would see him. Jeff returned to the shipping office knowing that his father was in his office and that Gilbert was in the back room. Praying that no customers would come in, Jeff approached Bobbie's desk.

"My dad tells me you're quitting."

Bobbie had of course seen him come in, and had waited quietly for him to take a seat. Jeff's plans to be completely alone with Bobbie for this confrontation went up in smoke. Discovering that she was quitting had sent him into something of a panic.

"I had to, Jeff. I know you understand."

"I understand a lot of things, but I'm not sure you do." Jeff spoke softly from the chair in front of the desk.

"I don't know what you're talking about."

"Then it's time you did. I think we have a lot to say to each other—things we should have discussed a long time ago."

Thinking he wanted her to continue working, Bobbie

gave him a negative shake of her head. "There's nothing to discuss, Jeff. Please just let me say what I need to say."

Jeff could see that she was not going to listen to reason until she could relate her feelings, so he folded his arms over his chest and waited.

"I know how upset you must be," Bobbie began, seeing she finally had his attention. "It was inexcusable of me to avoid you after what I did. I'm sorry, Jeff, for my behavior at the Walcotts', and I hope you'll forgive me. If you want, I can also apologize to Sylvia. If you'd rather I not mention it to her, I'll understand."

Something squeezed around Jeff's heart at the vulnerable way Bobbie sat across from him and bared her soul; her face and voice told of her misery. She was so precious to him, and she had done exactly what he feared—mentally chastised herself for days over a kiss he had thoroughly enjoyed.

Jeff was suddenly desperate to hold her hand and be near her, certain that if he did, his touch and words would put everything right. They had always touched in a special kind of way, and it never occurred to Jeff that such an action would not be welcome at the moment.

"Do you forgive me, Jeff?" His silence had brought Bobbie perilously close to tears. Jeff rose from his chair to circle the desk.

Bobbie, fearful that he would do just as he intended, and that his touch would be devastating to her emotions, sprang out of her own chair and moved around the desk to avoid him. "Jeff, please answer me."

"Just as soon as I get close enough, I'll answer you."

"Why when you're close?"

"Because I *need* to touch you, Bobbie," he answered as he followed her around the desk "And will you *please* hold still!"

The couple came to a stop where they had started, since they had completely circled the desk. Jeff thought this could go on all day, so before Bobbie could react he reached across the desktop and plucked the glasses from her nose.

"Jeff." The name was said fearfully, a sound that tugged at Jeff's heart, but he had to get this settled.

"It's all right, Bobbie," he said tenderly as he took her arm. "We're just going to head into the back room here so I can talk to you."

Bobbie was unaware of Gilbert leaving the room and closing the door behind him. She was led to the back of the room, where a small window cast a patch of sunlight on the wood floor.

When Bobbie felt a wall behind her, she leaned against it. In order to hide their trembling, she locked her hands together behind her back. Jeff still had her glasses, so until he leaned, with his forearm on the wall above her head, his face nose-to-nose with her own, she could not see him clearly.

"Will you kiss me again, Bobbie?" The question was whisper-soft and Bobbie searched Jeff's eyes for why he would be teasing her in this way.

"Why?" It was the only word that would come.

"Don't you want to?"

"You know I do." Bobbie's heart was in her eyes, and she did nothing to hide how wonderful it was to have Jeff so near. But it wasn't right. "Please don't torment me, Jeff. It's not like you to be cruel."

"I'm not doing a very good job with this, am I?" He said the words almost to himself, and Bobbie was more confused than ever.

"May I have my glasses?"

"Are you going to run away?"

"I might."

"Then no, you may not," he stated without moving. "And by the way, Sylvia left town this morning. She's headed home to stay."

Bobbie was silent, digesting this newest information.

"Now will you kiss me?"

"You want me to kiss you because Sylvia left town?" Bobbie felt like her world was spinning.

"No," Jeff said with great patience. "I want you to kiss me because you're going to be kissing me every day for the rest of our lives and we need the practice."

Bobbie's hands came up and grabbed frantically at the front of Jeff's shirt. "Please give me my glasses, Jeff."

He complied this time, and Bobbie searched Jeff's face from behind her lenses. 'This is why God told you to trust Him,' Bobbie said to herself as she clearly saw the love in Jeff's eyes.

"Why, Bobbie—why has it taken us so long to see what everyone else has seen for weeks?"

"I don't know," Bobbie answered, and truly she didn't. "Do you still want that kiss?"

Jeff's eyes narrowed with emotional fervor, and that was enough answer for Bobbie. Her hands framed either side of his face and she kissed him tenderly on the lips. Bobbie would have broken the kiss after a brief moment, but Jeff's arms had come around her, causing her own to slide without prompting around his neck. She returned his kiss with every drop of longing she had ever felt.

Bobbie was still a little dazed when Jeff stepped away from her with his hands on her shoulders.

"Don't kiss me like that again until after we're married."

Bobbie smiled. "And when will that be?"

"How's this evening?" The look on Jeff's face was so comical that Bobbie giggled. That laugh got her kissed again, and Gilbert, in the outer room, smiled at the silence.

"Why is the storeroom door shut?" Bill wanted to know as he exited the office.

"Jeff and Bob are in there."

"Are they talking?"

"Some of the time," Gil answered with a grin.

Bill looked at the closed portal and then back at his son. The two grinned at each other and Gilbert watched his father sigh with relief.

"It's about time, isn't it, Gilbert?"

The younger man's smile widened. "Yes, Dad, you're right. More than enough time."

forty-three

The hours after lunch evaporated in a dreamy haze for Bobbie. Jeff had a few errands to run and Bobbie made an effort to keep her mind on the job, but Gilbert repeated questions twice before she heard and she forgot the names of two customers. After the second such customer went out the door, Bobbie looked up to see Bill grinning at her. He had been uptown and had just come in.

"Jeff tells me you're staying." Father and son had run into each other outside the office and Jeff told his father of his plans.

"I *did* quit," Bobbie said almost hesitantly. "Did you hire someone else?"

Bill had no chance to answer because May shot in the door as if she had been chased by hounds.

"Oh Bobbie, Bobbie! I can't believe it. I just talked to Jeff and he told me. I didn't think he'd ever come to his senses!" Bobbie was enfolded in May's loving embrace, and over her shoulder Bobbie could see that Bill was still grinning.

"Bill!" May suddenly turned on her husband. "Why haven't you given this girl the day off? Why, she hasn't even had a chance to tell her family!"

"Well, I—" Bill started, but May cut him off.

"Now you just run along home, Bobbie; I'll fill in here. I can't think how Bill could have overlooked this."

Bobbie looked hesitant again, and May rushed on to assure her. "I'll tell Jeff you've gone home and I'm sure he'll be along shortly. We'll be fine for the rest of the day. Oh, here's Jeff now. Walk Bobbie home, dear, and then bring her to supper tonight. Ask Jake and Maryanne too."

"Can you believe this, Bill? First nothing, now two daughters-in-law and a grandchild..." May's words were cut off as she pushed the young couple out the front door and closed it behind them.

Bobbie and Jeff looked at each other and burst out laughing. "Your mother is wonderful."

"That she is. Did you really want to go home?"

"It wasn't my idea."

"Well, then, I'll have to thank my mother for the chance to have you all to myself."

They walked hand in hand toward the Bradfords', their conversation as relaxed as ever, but now with a certain intimacy that was both mysterious and exciting.

"The first question we're going to be asked tonight is *when*," Jeff told Bobbie.

"You mean, what date have we set?"

"That's it."

"Oh." Bobbie walked a few steps in silence. "What do we tell them?"

"Why, October fifth, of course!"

Bobbie came to a complete stop just before they walked into her yard. "You've already consulted a calendar?"

Jeff's look was adorably mischievous. "I've known for some time now that you were the one. Women aren't the only ones to plan and dream, you know. I didn't know when God would bring us together like He did today, but while I waited, I thought about our future constantly."

"I think I'm ready for you to tell me everything, like when you knew and all that."

"Well, I think I was pretty unsettled from the very beginning, since I was jealous of Gilbert when he ate lunch with you and I had to go to Sylvia's."

"Gilbert! Are you serious?"

"I'm afraid so, but that wasn't really the start. The start was when you came to the house to visit me after the accident. Remember when we played checkers?"

"I remember."

"I wanted to kiss your neck in the worst way."

"Jeff," Bobbie said softly, her cheeks heating just slightly, "that was weeks ago."

"I know, and all I can say is, God is a strong provider. You see, that was back when I still thought you might marry Cleve, and I knew I had no business feeling as I did, but God somehow moderated my feelings through that time.

"The *moderation* began to fade on the camping trip and evaporated completely when I felt your lips on mine."

Bobbie stared at him in amazement. "I knew something took place on the camping trip, but Jeff, the rest of what you said happened right after I came back to town."

"Yes, I know." Jeff smiled tenderly and bent to kiss her.

"I wondered when you two would get around to that," Troy interrupted the kissing couple. "I do hope this means you're going to marry her." Troy directed this question to Jeff, doing his best to look like an enraged father while a grin split his face.

"How does October fifth sound?"

"Great!" Troy exclaimed, and hugged his sister before shaking Jeff's hand. The three walked into the house and told Maryanne, who promptly erupted into tears. She couldn't speak for some moments.

"Oh Bobbie," she finally said, not caring that both Jeff and Troy were listening. "Please tell me it's love this time."

Bobbie looked to the tall, brown-haired man who quite literally held her heart in his grasp. Maryanne watched her daughter's eyes light with love, a love that matched the tender light in Jeff Taylor's eyes as he returned Bobbie's gaze.

"Never mind, Bobbie," she stopped her before she could speak. "You just put every fear to rest."

forty-four

October 5, 1872

Bobbie Taylor was helpless with laughter or she would have tried to reason with her captor.

"Now, Bobbie, just come along quietly," Rigg said in a voice as smooth as honey. "Let me tell you how much better you have it than my wife did. She was stuck in a cubicle at the church."

Rigg stopped before a bedroom on the upper floor at the Walcotts' and opened the door with confidence. Bobbie was amazed to see Gilbert inside.

"All right, Gil, here she is. I'll head back down and you see that she doesn't escape."

Rigg bent low and kissed his new sister-in-law's cheek. "Welcome to the family." Bobbie watched in silence as Rigg sailed back out the door. She turned on Gil as soon as the door shut.

"Gilbert Taylor! I can't believe you're a part of this!"

"I had to, Bobbie," he told her with a helpless smile.

"Rigg said if I didn't help I would *never* find my bride on my wedding day."

Bobbie truly sympathized with him and couldn't hold her laughter. "Where are you going?" She stopped when she saw Gilbert head for the door.

"I'm supposed to stand guard in the hallway."

Bobbie looked a little uncertain, and he stopped short of leaving the room.

"It's all right, Bobbie. I'll be right outside the door. Just make yourself comfortable."

Bobbie tried to do as she was told, but all she did was pace. They had chosen the room well, since the door Gilbert guarded was the only exit—unless she wanted to escape out a second-story window. She also noticed that the windows were all closed tight. Not that she would have shouted out one of them, but if Jeff began to look for her it would have been nice to wave at him from above.

Resigning herself to the circumstances, Bobbie finally did as Gil instructed. She sat in a chair and put her feet on a low stool. Within the space of a few minutes, she was sound asleep.

❑❑❑

"I've never seen a dress as beautiful as Bobbie's," Mrs. Walcott informed Jake. "But then I've never known a seamstress like your wife either."

"She has a real gift. And you, Mrs. Walcott, have a gift for generosity with your home. This is twice in the same year you've let us invade, and we thank you."

"Oh Jake," she said with a shake of her head, "you must know the pleasure's all mine. I'm a lonely old woman, and your Maryanne—well, let's just say this is a small thing in light of all she does for me."

They were joined by others, each complimenting Mrs. Walcott on her house and garden. Even though it was well into the fall, her yard was faithfully tended and still a showplace.

Jake listened with half an ear as Mrs. Walcott conversed. Having seen Rigg take Bobbie into the house and return without her, he had a keen premonition that Rigg was having one on the bridegroom. The thought made him smile, and at the same time he told himself he was not going to get involved, but he *was* going to keep his eyes open so not to miss any of the action.

❑❑❑

Rigg couldn't have asked for a better lead-in if he had planned it. He was holding Gretchen, looking to all the world as innocent as could be, when he joined his parents, Jeff, Maryanne, Troy, Carla, and his brother Nate. He listened to their conversation in silence until Bill asked where Bobbie had gone.

"I haven't seen her lately," Troy answered.

"I think she might have gone inside for something. Didn't I see her with you, Rigg?" The conversation went on so swiftly that no one immediately noticed that Rigg hadn't answered Maryanne's question.

Jeff was about to turn away from the group to look for his bride when he caught the slightest of smiles in his brother's eyes. Halting abruptly, Jeff leveled him with a stare.

"Rigg?" Jeff's voice was deep and serious.

"Yes, Jeffrey?" Rigg questioned him with a raise of his brow, and in that instant Jeff's suspicions stepped from doubt onto solid ground.

"Where is she?" Jeff asked, and tried not to smile. He noticed that Jake had suddenly joined the group, and his gaze swung to his new father-in-law, but Jake's look told Jeff he was not an accomplice.

"Where is Bobbie? You're not having trouble keeping track of your wife already, are you, Jeff?" Rigg was shocked. "Married these few hours and already apart? That's not a good start, Jeff old man, not good at all."

Rigg's words so closely echoed those of Jeff's at Rigg's wedding that the groom shouted with laughter.

"There's just one difference, Rigg," Jeff said through his chuckles. "If I know you, Bobbie is not going to escape from wherever you put her, as Kate did."

Rigg's grin was unrepentant, and Jeff had to do a good deal of negotiating, as well as put up with plenty of laughter and leg-pulling, to get Rigg to tell. When he finally had his answer, he started toward the house.

Rigg called after him, "Don't blame Gil; I threatened him into helping."

Rigg's words made complete sense to Jeff as soon as he hit the upstairs hallway. Gilbert was leaning calmly against the wall as though he was expecting Jeff, and he smiled as he approached. No words were exchanged as Gilbert took himself off to the party and Jeff let himself quietly into the bedroom.

Bobbie awoke when Jeff's lips touched her own. "Is that how boring you find our wedding day?"

Bobbie smiled drowsily, and Jeff scooped her into his arms, took her chair, and settled his new wife in his lap. Bobbie cuddled against him and Jeff stole another kiss.

"Do you know how long I've wanted to hold you like this?"

"I think so," Bobbie answered, and rested her head on Jeff's shoulder before she spoke again in a whisper.

"Have I been worth the wait?"

Jeff kissed her long and hard. "Does that answer your question?"

"Will you do that again?"

The groom smiled. "Well, I guess that answers *mine*."

Gilbert, who had come back upstairs to tell the newlyweds they were wanted in the garden, hesitated before knocking on the door of the silent room. A space of a few heartbeats passed and Gil shook his head in the empty corridor and started back downstairs. Bill met him on the landing.

"Did you talk to Jeff?"

"No, the door is shut and things are pretty quiet."

Bill remembered in a moment how much he had wanted to be alone with his wife after their wedding.

"I'm sure they'll come down soon. If not, Rigg can go up, since it's his fault Bobbie's up there in the first place."

Gilbert had no arguments with that line of reasoning and made a beeline for the food table. Bill, on the other hand, joined his wife, who asked where Jeff and Bobbie were.

"Newlyweds," was all Bill had to say as they walked arm in arm back to the party.

epilogue

Christmas Day 1872

The Taylor house was filled to the brim with family and friends. Bill, May, and sons were joined by Jake and Maryanne Bradford, Mr. Parker and Joey, the Marshall Riggs family, including Sean and Marcail Donovan, the Stuart Townsend family, Jeff and Bobbie Taylor, and Troy and Carla Bradford.

Bobbie was settled on the sofa with her niece Gretchen on her lap and her niece Paige at her side. When Marcail joined them, Bobbie laughed in delight at the smile that broke over Gretchen's face upon spotting her Aunt Marcail.

"Did you want to take her?"

"No, you can keep her. I get to hold her all the time. Will you have your own baby someday, Bobbie?"

"I hope so," Bobbie said with a smile that widened when her sister-in-law Carla stepped into the room. Bobbie simply could not picture her brother as a father, but it was going to happen in early spring.

Gretchen fussed a little and Bobbie transferred her onto her shoulder. With her tiny face cuddled into her aunt's neck, she soon fell asleep. The girls deserted Bobbie a few minutes later, and when Jeff saw the couch open next to his wife, he claimed the spot.

After quickly ducking his head so he could look beneath Bobbie's chin at his niece, Jeff kissed his wife's cheek.

"What was that for?"

"Do I need a reason to kiss my wife?"

"Definitely not," Bobbie answered, and this time offered her lips for his attention. They talked a few minutes before Sean joined them.

Bobbie smiled at the sight of him, since he was wearing the shirt that she and Jeff had given him for his sixteenth birthday, just a few weeks past.

"Are you up for a game of checkers, Jeff?" Sean looked desperate for a distraction of some type, and Jeff was compassionate.

"Sure," he answered easily. "Let's go into the kitchen." Sean kissed his niece's tiny head as he left the sofa. Watching them leave, Bobbie thought that Gretchen was probably the only person Sean Donovan was tender with at this time in his life. This was Sean's second Christmas without his father, and from the little Jeff had told her, she knew that he missed him desperately.

Bobbie had never experienced the troubled teen years that Sean was in the midst of, but also realized she had made the right choices. She prayed right on the spot that Sean would make wise choices, choices based on the good advice she knew he was getting from Rigg and Kaitlin.

He had worked all summer at the livery and that had basically kept him out of trouble, but he was running with a bad crowd again and wanted to quit school. Rigg had put his foot down, but Bobbie wondered when the top would blow sky-high.

Her thoughts were interrupted when Joey joined her and wanted to hold Gretchen. The transition woke her, but she didn't seem to mind. Bobbie and Joey both watched in fascination as she stretched and yawned, tiny fingers grasping in midair as her arms reached over her head.

"Isn't she cute?"

"She certainly is, Joey."

"Are you going to have a baby?"

'Twice in one hour,' Bobbie thought wryly, but answered nonetheless, "I'd like to."

"You'll have one if God wants you to, right?"

"Right." Bobbie answered with pleasure over Joey's insight. The time this young boy took each day to pray for his father's salvation was giving him a new perspective as to the way God deals with His children.

It wasn't long before Gretchen needed her mother and Joey ran off to find Wesley, Paige, and Marcail. Bobbie reached for a section of newspaper. The checkers game in the kitchen did not last long, and before Bobbie expected, Jeff was back at her side.

"That was fast."

"Sean was preoccupied."

Bobbie nodded and was silent. She glanced up to see Jeff watching Carla. "I could look like that one of these days."

"That's quite true."

"Will you still want to hold me?"

"Definitely," he said as his arm went around her. Bobbie liked the way he said that, without a moment's hesitation.

"Dinner is served," May called from the doorway a moment later. "Everyone find a seat."

There was general pandemonium while everyone was seated either in the kitchen or living room. When all was quiet, Bill stood in the doorway between the two rooms and returned thanks for the food.

"Our Father in heaven, we thank You for the food on these tables and the hands that worked to provide and prepare it. We also thank You for the miracle of grandchildren and their presence with us today. We praise You for Bobbie, as well as the extended family she brings along, and for friends that You bring us in Your time.

"And lastly we thank You for this season and the birth of Your Son. May we be mindful of Your love, a love so great that You gave Your only Son to us. May we remember to keep You before us, today and all days. Amen."

Bill's gaze slowly encompassed the two rooms. He was met with smiles and some tears as he beamed in love at all beneath his roof.

About the Author

Lori Wick is one of the most versatile Christian fiction writers on the market today. From pioneer fiction to a series set in Victorian England to contemporary writing, Lori's books (over 1 million copies in print) are perennial favorites with readers. *The Californians* series is a heartwarming tale of lives in the care of a sovereign God.

Born and raised in Santa Rosa, California, Lori met her husband, Bob, while in Bible college. They and their three children, Timothy, Matthew, and Abigail, make their home in Wisconsin.

About the Author

Lori Wick is one of the most versatile Christian fiction writers on the market today. Her works include pioneer fiction, a series set in Victorian England, and contemporary novels. Lori's books (over 1.5 million copies in print) continue to delight readers and top the Christian bestselling fiction list. Lori and her husband, Bob, live in Wisconsin with "the three coolest kids in the world."

Books by Lori Wick

A Place Called Home Series

A Place Called Home
A Song for Silas
The Long Road Home
A Gathering of Memories

The Californians

Whatever Tomorrow Brings
As Time Goes By
Sean Donovan
Donavan's Daughter

Kensington Chronicles

The Hawk and the Jewel
Wings of the Morning
Who Brings Forth the Wind
The Knight and the Dove

Rocky Mountain Memories

Where the Wild Rose Blooms
Whispers of Moonlight
To Know Her by Name
Promise Me Tomorrow

The Yellow Rose Trilogy

Every Little Thing About You

Contemporary Fiction

Sophie's Heart
Beyond the Picket Fence (Short Stories)
Pretense
The Princess

Harvest House Publishers

For the Best in Inspirational Fiction

Linda Chaikin

TRADE WINDS
Captive Heart
Silver Dreams
Island Bride

A DAY TO REMEMBER
Monday's Child

Virginia Gaffney

THE RICHMOND CHRONICLES
Under the Southern Moon
Magnolia Dreams

Maryann Minatra

THE ALCOTT LEGACY
The Masterpiece

LEGACY OF HONOR
Before Night Falls

Lisa Samson

THE HIGHLANDERS
The Highlander and His Lady
The Legend of Robin Brodie

G. Roger Corey

In A Mirror Dimly
Eden Springs

Melody Carlson

A Place to Come Home to